THE KYTOS PROJECT

THE KYTOS PROJECT

The Rathing Chronicles

John von Kesmark

Book Guild Publishing
Sussex, England

First published in Great Britain in 2006 by
The Book Guild Ltd
Pavilion View
19 New Road
Brighton, East Sussex
BN1 1UF

Typesetting in Verdana by
SetSystems Ltd, Saffron Walden, Essex

Printed in Great Britain by
CPI Bath

A catalogue record for this book is
available from the British Library

ISBN 1 84624 047 6

Cyte: a mature cell

The word is derived from the Greek *kytos*,
meaning "hollow"

Shi'bbolĕth:

Old-fashioned doctrine or formula of party or sect

It would be remiss of me if I did not acknowledge all those who have given me every encouragement and support. Their patience and advice has been invaluable. Many have lived with the exploits of Rathings and Magars for a considerable time.

So, I say thank you to my wife Diane for her constructive criticism, for correcting my grammar and for keeping the world at bay during my writing sessions.

To my sons Paul and Carl, and to Louise for their incisive observations and suggestions on the direction the story should take.

To Elaine, Mary and Angela for their help. To Chris Morris for advice on genetic engineering and other cloning technologies, and to Kate, who read my first draft and whose enthusiastic response encouraged me to go on and complete the story.

And not least, my gratitude to Joanna Bentley and Robert Anderson, managing editor and copy-editor respectively, for doing a sterling job and to the rest of the management, creative and publicity teams at Book Guild Publishing for their professional approach and hard work.

The Kytos Project is truly a team effort.

To you all, I am very grateful.

John von Kesmark

Old Isleworth, Middlesex, England
2006

Ah, the wonder of it. To be neither wholly man nor beast, fish nor fowl, but a chimera of Man's own creation. This is not fantasy because fantasy is fanciful speculation. This is a scientific reality. My new breed of creatures is living proof of Man's capability to create new forms of life and sets Man on the same pedestal as the Almighty Creator.

Professor Jens Andersen
The Kytos Project Lecture, May 2016

PRINCIPAL CHARACTERS

The Humans

Jack – *A schoolboy, whose two friends are –*
Ashok
Bill
Jimmy – *A rough, tough bully of a teenager*
Doctor Pierre Fournier – *A slave-prisoner*
Harry Carter – *Rebel leader of the Freedom Fighters*

The Rathings

Vadek – *Overlord of Cornwall*
General Garbath – *Vadek's brother and military com-
    mander in Cornwall*
Panuf – *High Priest and Keeper of the Scrolls*
Commanders Mordon, Xander and Kera – *Corps
    commanders*
Federus – *Leader of the Supreme Council*
Darma – *Member of the Supreme Council*

The Magars

Horos
Rough Bird

THE RATHING CAVE NETWORK AT RUMRUNNER COVE

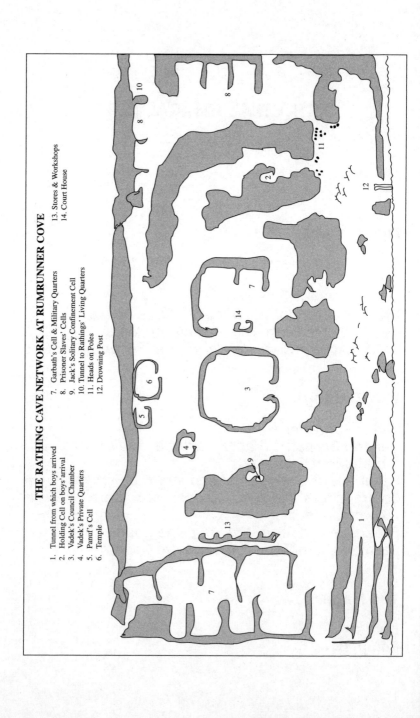

1. Tunnel from which boys arrived
2. Holding Cell on boys' arrival
3. Vadek's Council Chamber
4. Vadek's Private Quarters
5. Panuf's Cell
6. Temple

7. Garbath's Cell & Military Quarters
8. Prisoner Slaves' Cells
9. Jack's Solitary Confinement Cell
10. Tunnel to Rathings' Living Quarters
11. Heads on Poles
12. Drowning Post

13. Stores & Workshops
14. Court House

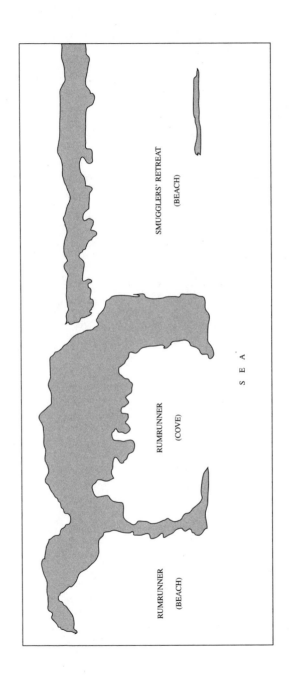

RUMRUNNER
(BEACH)

RUMRUNNER
(COVE)

SMUGGLERS' RETREAT
(BEACH)

S E A

They took Jimmy to the torture chamber.

All kinds of wicked-looking instruments lined the cave walls: pliers, hacksaws, hammers, whips, sharp, pointed metal skewers and many more. A fire blazed in a brazier standing against one of the walls.

They tied him to the floor with heavy chains. A hard-muscled very large black-furred Rathing, standing over three metres tall, approached, holding a pair of pliers in his massive paws. Jimmy could not help noticing that the Rathing's human feet with rat toes were badly scarred and very dirty.

"Well, putrid, smelly human," the Rathing said, turning towards Jimmy, his eyes red pinpricks of hatred staring from his rat face, "do you want your fingernails or your toenails pulled out first, before we boil you alive?"

Jimmy was so frightened he gagged and was nearly sick. He was desperate to delay the impending torture. In an effort to do so, he let out a strangulated cry, rolled his eyes upwards till the whites showed, and his head flopped to one side as if he had fainted. He held his breath and waited.

His trick had worked.

He heard the big Rathing swear. "Take him away," the Rathing ordered. "He can't enjoy the pain unless

1

he is fully conscious. Let him lie awake tonight imagining what waits in store for him." The Rathing torturer gave a deep chuckle of pleasure at the thought of the various ways he could inflict pain on the boy.

The anticipated delights produced dribbles of grey-green saliva from his foul-smelling mouth.

1

Jack and his parents watched the news on television and listened intently to what the controversial news-caster and commentator "Chuck" Gordon was say-ing: "Our glorious President Axel has issued a communiqué from Rathing Palace to the effect that negotiations with the United Nations and the United States of America to rescind the embargo against the Democratic Republic of Britain are proceeding satisfactorily. It is expected that an early agreement will be reached."

Jack's mum clapped her hands in delight. "Wouldn't it be wonderful? The shops will have such a variety of fruit and vegetables and other foodstuff from abroad. It'll be like the old days again."

"Shh!" Jack's dad said. "There's a bit more."

"Chuck" Gordon was speaking: ". . . to have with us in the studio the Leader of the Rathings' Council, Supreme Leader Federus. Supreme Leader Federus, I should like to ask you if you may know when any agreement will be definitely finalised."

"No," the Rathing replied.

"Is it weeks or months, or perhaps even longer?"

"I gave you my answer."

The curt reply did not best please Chuck. It was his job to extract information from interviewees for a news-hungry population. He liked to be provocative; it helped boost the station's ratings. Yet, he was conscious that his ultimate masters were the Rathings, and he had to tread a careful balance so as to not appear disrespectful.

"Our glorious President's communiqué states that it is expected that an early agreement will be reached. May I respectfully say that we've heard this before? It's been many decades since Britain was isolated from the worldwide community. Can you perhaps enlighten us? Is there anything further you wish to add?" The newsman gave Federus an encouraging smile, hoping the fat Rathing might be inclined to say more than half a dozen words.

As Federus leant back in his seat, Chuck was surprised to realise that he was quite small by Rathing standards, measuring a mere two metres. He also noted that the dark blue leather jerkin and leather kilt, the accepted dress code for civilian Rathings, were bulging around the Rathing's broad frame and that the creature was finding it difficult to fit into the chair.

Federus's tiny eyes looked at him condescendingly from a bloated face. The rat fur all over his body was grey, although streaks of white were visible in certain parts.

"You have heard this said before because it is our policy always to be open and informative with you humans. If other nations wish to procrastinate then you should perhaps direct your question to the President of the United States of America and the Secretary General of the United Nations. Our glorious President continues to make great headway in his talks with other world leaders. It is his desire that the Rathing Nation be accepted as a member of the worldwide community and that we can take our rightful place in the commonwealth of nations. It is our hope that international trade and travel can commence soon after agreements are ratified. We have borne with fortitude the isolation enforced on us. We also speak for the Magars, who are ostracised by the outside world. Both we and the Magars are clones created by man. It is the duty of humans to accept us for what we are. It has always been our desire to peacefully co-exist with the human population throughout the world. We have already shown this by our behaviour to you humans in the Democratic Republic of Britain, would you not agree?"

Chuck looked down at his desk and fumbled with some papers. Broadcasters are not generally encouraged to agree or disagree with any question put to them. He therefore continued, "Rathings have ruled the British Isles for a long time and we humans are grateful for being allowed to carry on our lives pretty well much as before.

"You say you speak also for the Magars. But the Magars are only another set of inhabitants. And they have no power, no say in government. They wouldn't be interested in, or indeed able to enter into, trade agreements as they have nothing to trade with. They have no military force or leaders. They are disenfranchised. How would they be affected? "

Federus adjusted himself in his chair for the umpteenth time. He looked distinctly uncomfortable. "I accept that the Magars are another set of inhabitants. They hold no power because they are savages with no religion or hierarchical society as we have. We have tried to introduce religion to the Magars, to convert them to worshipping God Andersen. Regrettably, they are resistant to our overtures. Neverthe-

5

less, they, too, are clones and we acknowledge their rights to share in the good fortune we shall soon enjoy. If Magars are incapable of doing so it would not be for want of our trying to make these opportunities available to them. Our glorious President is confident of success."

"Thank you, Supreme Leader Federus. We are pleased to know that our glorious President is confident of progress." Chuck gave a sickly smile. "The hopes and good wishes of everyone in the Republic of Britain are with you."

"Let me assure you, Mr Gordon, and all your viewers, that negotiations are going well. Our nation now stands at the crossroads of her destiny."

Chuck smiled at the politician's oft-used sound bite. Yah, yah, yah, a new era now dawns, etcetera, etcetera, he thought to himself. He said, "We await the outcome with bated breath," before realising that he too had trotted out a similar well-worn cliché.

"All hail to our glorious President," Federus said, placing his right paw against his left breast.

"All hail to our glorious President," the newsman mumbled before turning to another camera and saying, "And now for the rest of the news . . ."

"Bedtime I think, Jack," his mum said. "You need to get a good night's sleep if you're going to be out all day tomorrow with your friends."

Jack's dad rose from his chair. "I'll get a packed lunch ready for you to take. Playing cricket on the beach can be thirsty work – and famishing too!" He turned to his wife who started to get up. "No, you stay there, darling. I'll do it."

"Thanks, Dad." Jack gave his father a huge smile.

6

Jack's mum leant forward and asked softly, "Can you manage the stairs or would you like your father to carry you up?"

Jack shook his head and raised himself slowly from his chair. "No, Mum. I'm fine. I can manage."

She walked over to Jack and kissed his forehead. "Good night, love. Sleep tight . . ."

". . . And don't let the bedbugs bite," Jack added with a despairing look. Mum was so predictable. He sometimes thought his mother treated him like a three-year-old. Just because I'm physically incapacitated doesn't mean I'm mentally senile, he said to himself. He turned to his father, "'Night, Dad."

"Good night, son," his dad said and gave him a playful, very light punch on the arm.

2

The sun beat down on Rumrunner Beach where the three boys were enjoying the last few days of their summer holiday playing cricket.

For the first time in many days Jack was feeling well. His spirits were high. His body seemed light and free, as if it were floating on a giant marshmallow. He felt good. The dark clouds of despondency that sometimes hung around him were lifted.

He leant forward in his wheelchair and raised his right hand and index finger. "Out!" he cried.

"No way!" Bill threw down his bat in disgust. "The ball hit the sand first."

Ashok strolled over, a big grin sketched across his face. He playfully tossed the cricket ball from one hand to the other. "Look here, old man. Mustn't argue with the umpire," he drawled, putting on a plummy, posh accent, "Not cricket, old boy."

"Too right it's not cricket!" Bill kicked at his dropped bat. "It's unfair, that's what it is. Look, Ashok," he pleaded, "I'm not saying you're cheating or anything like that. But you got it wrong. The ball definitely just touched the sand as you dived to catch it. I saw it clearly."

"What d'you say, umpire?" Ashok looked at Jack with questioning eyebrows.

"Well, in case of any uncertainty the benefit of the doubt does go to the batsman," Jack smiled. "Guess you've got another life, Bill."

Bill once again took his stance in front of the wicket. Jack smiled to himself as he noted the determined look that stamped itself on Bill's plump face. Jack knew that Bill sometimes took things too seriously, but this was only a game for goodness sake! He watched Bill ready himself, thumping the bat several times into the sand as he waited for Ashok to bowl. Bill hit the next delivery with a resounding thump. The cricket ball sailed high into the air, landed close to the cliff face and rolled the last few metres into the cave mouth.

"Hey, that was a great hit, Bill!" Jack exclaimed. "I'd say six."

"I'll get it," Ashok shouted and ran towards the cliff.

Jack leant back in his wheelchair and looked up at the blue sky. He was a slim, very good-looking boy of eleven with dark-brown hair, the front of which always flopped across his brow. His soft, hazel-coloured eyes showed a great intelligence and strength of character but, if one bothered to look deeper, they also often portrayed a great sadness. But today his eyes sparkled with happiness. He gave a big sigh of contentment. If only every day felt as good as this, he thought, life would be really, really great. He listened to the waves slapping insolently against the rocks.

A few seagulls pirouetted overhead, their screeches sounding like cheers at Bill's massive hit. They seem happy as well, Jack thought.

"Hey you lot! I can see what you're up to." The shout wrenched Jack from his reverie.

He turned and saw a figure sauntering towards them.

"Oh, no!" he muttered to himself. "It's Jimmy Nelson."

Jimmy was older than the others were. He was fourteen and went to the local high school. He was a Londoner and had only recently moved to Cornwall with his parents because of his stepdad's job with the Highways Department of the local Council.

Jimmy swaggered up to Jack and poked him in the chest. "Listen 'ere, Cripple. No one's allowed in there. That cave leads to Rumrunner Cove. It's a no-go area and you know it, sunshine."

Jack gripped the arms of his wheelchair and looked up at the older and bigger boy who leaned over him. Jimmy's hard and square face was pitted with pimples. His breath stank, and Jack turned his face away slightly to avoid inhaling the fetid air. Jimmy mistook Jack's move as a sign of fear. "Scared you've been caught out, eh?" he laughed.

In truth, Jack *was* nervous of Jimmy's belligerent attitude. Jimmy revelled in his reputation amongst both children and adults of being the village bully. Few people realised that Jimmy had never been engaged in more than a handful of fights. His sup-posed reputation as a hard man had grown only from his aggressive, hostile attitude. This suited him fine and he meant to keep this image of himself intact until a bigger and stronger lad came along, some-thing that Jimmy hoped would never happen.

"Ashok is just going to get our cricket ball back. It's only at the mouth of the cave," Jack explained.

Ashok, who was twelve years old, strode purpose-fully back towards the group and headed straight towards Jimmy. He looked the older boy straight in the eye. "What's with you? Get a life or get lost. This has nothing to do with you."

Ashok knew of Jimmy's reputation, but he was confident that if it came to a fight with the bigger boy, he'd be able to take him on quite easily.

Jimmy clenched his fist and looked directly into Ashok's very dark eyes, trying unsuccessfully to out-stare him. The younger boy was almost as tall as he was and Jimmy noted Ashok's broad shoulders and strong, muscular body. Ashok's slightly crooked nose, broken several times in rugby matches, did nothing to mar his good looks; if anything, it went down well with the girls at school as it gave him an even tougher and more mature look. The boys confronted each other like two warring stags, neither prepared to back down.

"Who d'you think you're talking to, greaseball?" Jimmy snarled, annoyed at Ashok's manner. Jimmy reckoned that Ashok would be no pushover in a fight. He didn't really feel inclined to test out this theory. Yet he was certainly not prepared to have the younger lad stand up to him.

Bill sensed trouble brewing. He moved in quickly between the two boys. "Hey, hey, let's keep it together, eh?" he said in a placating voice. "We're only playing cricket."

Jimmy, confronted by both Ashok and Bill, moved back a step and put his hands in the pockets of his jeans. He grinned at Jack.

"Lost your ball then, have we?" he said in a sing-song voice

"No, mate. It's right here," Ashok said, pushing the retrieved cricket ball under Jimmy's nose.

"Can we get on with our game now?" Bill asked, indicating with his head that Jimmy should move off.

11

Jimmy shrugged. "S'pose so. How can you play cricket with just three people?" He inclined his head to the side as he tended to do when asking a question. It was one of his strange mannerisms. "Go on. Gis a game then. I bet I can hit the ball further than you did, fat boy."

The three other boys exchanged nervous glances. None of them particularly liked Jimmy. Jack thought that the whole manner of their game would change once Jimmy was involved. But he felt that it would be rude and hurtful to refuse, so he said, "OK."

Jimmy shook his head. "Nah, I'm not playing with a bunch of kids. I was just testing you out, like."

He turned and sauntered away, kicking at the sand, and sat further along the beach.

None of the boys felt like continuing their game. They stood around for a while. Then Ashok whispered, "Hey, let's really get up that silly sod's nose. Let's pretend we're going to go into the cave."

Jack gave a slight frown. "I don't know about that. And Jimmy was right. We're not allowed to go there."

"I'm not suggesting we go right through. Just stand inside the entrance where we can't be seen so he thinks we've made our way right into the cave."

Jack, still in high spirits, said, "OK, then. Just for a laugh."

Bill scratched his mop of blond hair and grimaced. Beads of perspiration glistened on his round face. His sweaty appearance was due more to being unnerved at the recent confrontation than to the hot sun. Bill liked to enjoy a quiet, peaceful life with no untoward situations arising. "I don't like the idea. It could be dangerous," he said.

"We're only standing in the entrance, for crying

out loud!" Ashok exclaimed. "Come on, Bill, be a little adventurous." Ashok laughed loudly. "Live dangerously."

Ashok began to push Jack's wheelchair towards the cave. Bill dawdled behind. They gave a perfunctory glance at the wooden noticeboard at the cave entrance that read:

KEEP OUT
RATHING CIVIL & MILITARY ESTABLISHMENT
ENTRY FORBIDDEN

Ashok shoved aside the coil of barbed wire and lifted one of the wooden barriers so as to gain access. He wheeled Jack towards the entrance and the three boys entered the semi-dark, cool cave. The white sand was slightly wet from sea water that had flowed in and had remained damp due to the absence of any sunshine. They saw several tiny crabs dashing about, as if seeking shelter from the intrusion by the boys. Ashok continued to push Jack further down the cave tunnel whilst Bill followed somewhat reluctantly.

Jack couldn't see what the problem would be if they did indeed go all the way through to the mouth of the cave overlooking Rumrunner Cove. He had never experienced any difficulties with the Rathings that he came across in his village. Sure, they were the bosses who ruled the place, but so long as humans gave them no trouble, the Rathings left everyone alone. Jack believed that Jimmy was just being annoying in telling them off about the cave. Jack and Ashok were getting carried away with the enthusiasm of doing something daring, by being a little bit more adventurous than usual. With spirits still high, Jack laughed aloud, swung his right arm forward in an arc and called out, "Onward, slave driver! Do not tarry." Ashok joined in Jack's laughter and pushed the wheelchair further into the tunnel.

3

Jimmy watched them enter the cave. What bozos, he thought. They'll get some real agro if the Rathings find them in that cave. He grinned at the thought of the repercussions.

After a few minutes, curiosity got the better of him and he decided to follow.

Jimmy liked the coolness of the cave, which was so refreshing after the stifling heat on the beach. Although the others were some way ahead it was easy to follow their tracks.

Jack's wheelchair and the others' footprints left clear marks in the damp sand. Jimmy crept on, his ears straining to pick up any sounds. But it was deathly silent. He followed the tracks and reached a point where two side tunnels branched off from the main cave. He noticed footprints and wheel tracks travelling in a straight direction, as if continuing down the centre tunnel. They then turned back on themselves, returned to the crossroads, and then slewed to the right hand tunnel where they obviously stopped, as the sand was all churned up. Jimmy could almost imagine the group's uncertainty as they debated which path to take. Eventually the tracks veered and went down the tunnel to the left. He wondered what had made them change their minds and decide on this particular route. And what had prompted them to go all the way into the cave.

The gloomy silence was beginning to make Jimmy feel uneasy. He had always felt uncomfortable in situations that he could not control. He walked on, more slowly now, and debated with himself whether it would not be more sensible to turn back and return to more familiar territory.

Then he saw the distant sun's rays shining through the far entrance of the cave and the silhouettes of the others framed in the mouth of the cave exit. He breathed a sigh of relief and stumbled towards them.

Jack sat in his wheelchair with Ashok and Bill on either side of him. They slowly took in the view and marvelled at the sight before them. They had always envisaged Rumrunner Cove as being small, as coves usually are. But this beach was larger than they had imagined. They were struck by the wide vista that lay before them.

To their right, the sea glittered like a sheer sheet of blue-green glass, the sun's rays sparkling off its surface. The clear green water near the shore gradually turned a deep blue further out. A range of sand dunes, topped by occasional clumps of tussocks, began some distance away to their left. High cliffs, rugged, dark brown and yellowish in colour, towered above the cave entrance in which they stood. The cliffs continued to both left and right of them in a horseshoe shape up to the shoreline as if enfolding the cove in a hard embrace. The air was hot and still. The heat created a shimmering effect on the sand so that it seemed to wave and dance before their eyes. At the farthest point there appeared to be dozens of long poles stuck in the sand with an object skewered on the top of each pole. It was difficult to make out from that distance what they were.

"What d'you think those things are?" Bill pointed. "They look a bit strange."

The silence was palpable. "Notice anything else that's odd?" Ashok asked.

The others shook their heads.

"There are no gulls perched on the cliffs. None swooping over the sea or flying about. No bird sounds. Just dead silence."

"That's possibly because the Magars live up there," Jack said.

They were very aware of the total stillness around them. Even the sea was placid, dead calm and the few small waves that trickled on to the beach were muted. A warm breeze kissed their faces with sound-less lips. Nothing stirred. Nothing sounded.

They peeked out further and looked up at the cliffs towering immediately above them.

Ashok clambered down on to the beach and glanced around. "Well, I can't see what's so special or secret about this cove. It's just like any other beach."

"Not quite," Jack pointed towards the caves at the far end. "That's the headquarters of the Rathing Overlord. Funny that no one seems to be around."

Ashok pointed to the side of the cliff where they stood. "Look, could those be footprints?"

He moved towards the cliff face and squatted down to study the marks in the sand. "You know, I think they are. They're human footprints. And it looks like they've been made recently."

Bill carefully pushed Jack's wheelchair down the incline. The heat on the sand was so intense that

Ashok and Bill felt it through the soles of their trainers.

Jack began to doubt the wisdom of their decision to go through the cave. "I think we should get out of here before we find ourselves in trouble."

"That's what I said in the first place," Bill moaned.

The silence was broken by a hoarse, loud whisper from close by.

"Oi! You lot! Over here! Quick!"

They turned, startled at the sound. An oldish man, unshaven and with long white hair, was crouching behind some rocks. He beckoned with frantic signals. He wore a dirty bandage over his eyes.

"Quick, quick! Come here! It's dangerous standing out in the open."

The boys were dumbfounded. They had hardly expected to see anyone else on the seemingly deserted and forbidden beach and they were frightened by his strange behaviour. What could he be doing on this beach where no one was allowed? And why was he acting so dramatically? They moved hesitantly towards him.

"Get a move on!" he called out tersely. "Get behind these rocks."

At that, they hurried towards him and the shelter of the rocks. Jack wished that Bill and Ashok didn't push his wheelchair with such speed towards the stranger. The man was naked to the waist and wore no socks or shoes. His chest, shoulders and arms were nearly black from suntan and muscles like whipcord rippled as he moved. He might look old but there was no doubt that he was supremely fit.

"What the devil are you doing here?" the man demanded.

Jimmy had by now also clambered down to the

beach and heard the man's question. He stood with his arms on his hips, legs akimbo.

"Whas it got to do with you, sunshine?" Jimmy said loudly.

The old man whispered urgently, "Look, boy. If you value your life I hope you're not standing where you can be seen."

Jimmy sneered. "Oh yeah, says who?" He stuck his chin forward and looked at the man aggressively.

The man turned towards the others. "Will you tell that damned fool friend of yours to hide."

Bill signalled to Jimmy. "Come on. You'd better get over here." He then turned to the man and voiced the question they all had. "Why are you on this beach, sir? It's the Rathings headquarters. We thought no one's allowed here."

"I might ask the same of you," the man snapped.

Jimmy lolled over nonchalantly, hands in pockets, to join the others who crouched besides the man.

"What are you doing here?" Ashok demanded.

"Wha?"

"I said why are you here?"

"Followed you, didn' I."

The man put a finger to his lips, indicating silence. His face was gaunt and several days' growth of beard, brown and with specks of white, peppered his cheeks and chin. "This isn't the time or place to enter into arguments," he whispered. "I'm trying to make my way through the cave from this cove onto Rum-runner Beach on the other side. Come on, you can lead me there. We must all leave this place. Before any Rathings turn up."

"Excuse me," Jack said. "Can't you see properly?"

The man gave a rueful smile. "I can't see at all. I have no eyes."

19

4

Jack was about to make some appropriate comment when he saw what appeared to be giant gliders launching themselves from the cliff top and come hurtling down towards the beach. As they neared the beach, the children realised that these flying objects were not gliders but a group of Magars. These enormous creatures had the black head, white torso and bright blue wings of a magpie but possessed a human body from the waist down, apart from a magpie tail. Thick plumage covered their entire body.

The four boys stood in surprise, watching these strange apparitions land on the sand and hurry towards them, their heads twitching nervously, tails bobbing up and down and eyes darting about, scanning every part of the beach. They knew, of course, of the existence of the Magars and had seen pictures of them, but very few people had seen them in the flesh, as Magars were inclined to live on cliff tops and rarely, if ever, entered towns or villages. Seeing a real, live Magar for the first time was an unnerving experience.

"What's happening?" the man asked nervously.

"Some Magars have arrived," Jack explained.

There was a sudden commotion and loud squeaks

coming from the caves ahead of them. The boys turned in fright.

Streaming towards them were several Rathings. They carried spears and swords, as well as rifles.

"What's happening now?" the man demanded.

"Rathings," Jack said in a frightened voice.

"Oh, Lord," the man groaned. "I've had it now."

The Magars had now turned and began to attack the advancing Rathings. Jack was terrified at the chaos around him. The Magars were large, all being at least two metres in height, but they were over-shadowed by the taller Rathings, most of whom stood over three metres. One of the Magars who stood next to Jack fell down, shot dead. Jack noticed that despite this one casualty by gunfire, the Rathings seemed to be poor shots as they missed most of their targets. Other Magars overwhelmed the rifle-carrying Rathings and tore them to bits with their sharp beaks and talons. The two sets of giant mutant clones were having a ferocious fight. More Magars now arrived, swooping down from the cliff top. Some of the Magars surrounded the children and the old man, forming a protective ring around them. Jack couldn't see very much. His view was obscured by the mass of feathered clones standing beside his wheelchair.

The initial attack force of Rathings had seemingly rushed out in a hurry because they were totally unprotected apart from the few weapons they carried. As the Magars moved about him, Jack managed to peek past their huge bodies and saw a further contingent of Rathings rush onto the beach. Unlike the earlier arrivals who had worn no clothes, these were dressed in leather tunics and short leather skirts. Some had long leather thongs that hung from shoulder to chest. They held shields as well as lances, swords and guns. They advanced slowly, and as they did so they began to place their shields to their sides and above their heads, forming a protective carapace of metal. Long lances poked out from between the gaps of the shields, making it impossible for the Magars to find any vulnerable areas to attack. Other Rathings, behind the advancing force, opened fire with their guns but, again, their abysmal marksmanship enabled the Magars to continue their attack.

Jack watched as a huge, broad-chested Rathing with an eyepatch was surrounded by more than a dozen Magars. His leather outfit was dyed a deep red and he was wielding his sword skilfully and swiftly despatched each Magar in turn. As more Magars attacked him, they too were slaughtered. He looked tremendously strong and more than capable of taking on the entire force of Magars.

The Rathings, with their array of weapons and superior size and numbers were gaining the upper hand. The group was now completely encircled.

A Magar tucked the man under one wing and flew upwards, propelling itself with only its other large, strong wing. Another did the same to Ashok, who was the nearest one of the group standing besides the man. Other Magars attempted to get hold of the rest but were beaten back by the now large group of Rathings.

Some Rathings fired into the air and missed. Another threw his spear at the old man as he was being lifted into the air. It pierced his side and he let out a scream of pain.

The Magars, apart from those who lay dead or dying, made their escape to the cliff top.

It was too late to save Jack, Bill and Jimmy. The

Rathings surrounded them and held spears at their chests.

Jack's heart was beating with terror. He closed his eyes and grasped tightly at the arms of his wheel-chair. A surge of panic gripped him and he felt sick. He trembled and prayed that none of the Rathings would decide to pierce him with a spear. He did not want to die.

The heat from the hot summer sun was almost unbearable. Jack's throat was very dry, so dry in fact, that he hardly had any saliva to swallow. He began to feel faint. The cloying, rancid smell of the surrounding Rathings nearly made him gag. He had never before been so very close to any of these creatures.

He glanced up towards where Bill and Jimmy had been standing. Bill's face was ashen white, his blue eyes round as saucers. He was biting ferociously at his fingernails. Jimmy lay in a heap on the sand. Jack hoped that he had fainted and not been killed. Then Jack breathed a sigh of relief as he saw Jimmy slowly sit up and rub his shaven head nervously.

One of the Rathings moved away from the rest and approached the cowering children. A frayed, dirty red blanket was draped around his shoulders, and he wore a short light-brown leather kilt. He held a long, bloodied spear in his right paw, the shaft of which rested on the sand. Pure white fur covered his ratlike upper body as well as his human thighs and legs. His rat face was long and thin, his eyes sharp and pink. He bore all the characteristics of an albino rat.

The children recognised him as Vadek, the local Overlord. His picture had appeared on many posters displayed from time to time in the towns and villages.

Vadek looked down from his great height. "I am Vadek," he announced, "Overlord and leader of my tribe. What are you doing here? You know it is forbidden for humans to venture onto this cove."

His voice was deep, his diction perfect, if rather condescending. He sounded self-assured and arrogant.

He looked down at Jack. "Why have you come here?" he demanded.

Jack was too terrified to speak. The enormous half-rat, half-human who stood before him glared threateningly.

"I asked you a question!" Vadek's tone was sharp and angry.

Jack gulped and whispered, "We, er, we, we got lost in the cave from our beach."

Bill and Jimmy stood close to each other for reassurance and nodded their heads vigorously in agreement.

Vadek kicked lightly at Jack's wheelchair. "You are lying."

He turned to one of his companions. "Lock these intruders in the holding cell," he ordered. "We shall put them with the slave labour force."

5

Bill pushed Jack's wheelchair as the group was escorted along the beach towards some distant caves. They looked up apprehensively at the huge figures of the six Rathing guards who surrounded them. No one spoke. They eventually reached the caves in front of which stood the long poles. As they neared the caves they were horrified to see that the objects skewered on top of each pole were skulls. Some of them were quite small, almost as if they had belonged to children. Most were bleached white by the sun, but others retained some bloated and discoloured flesh, a few with greyish skin hanging in strips as decomposition set in. The eye sockets were empty, yet seemed to be accusatory in their blank-ness. Tufts of feathers or human hair sprouted on some of the skulls. Overriding this desolate, gothic scene was the stench of putrefying flesh. One of the Rathings escorting the children noticed them staring up at the poles. He pointed at the heads. "Magars' heads," he stated with a smile. His accent, unlike Vadek's, held a trace of unknown dialect and he spoke in a much quieter, yet gruff, voice. "Our enemies killed in battle or captured and put to death. They are placed there to serve as a warning to all Magars to accept that they can never beat us, that one day we shall destroy them totally." Then indicating the few human heads, he said, "Those were human slaves who outlived their use. And the little heads are those of Droons."

Jack wondered what the Rathing meant by the people having outlived their use. He felt sick to hear that people were executed in such a manner. And he was even sicker at the thought that he and the other boys were to be put with the labour force. Jack knew that the Rathings periodically launched raids in towns and villages to conscript humans as slave labour, but the Rathings had never captured children; they regarded youngsters as unsuitable to cope with the hard work.

Jack felt the heavy cloak of despondency settle itself around his shoulders. He doubted he'd ever see his mum and dad again. He and the others were to disappear from their family and friends, forced to work for the Rathings. He wondered what kind of work these creatures had in mind for them.

The boys were led into one of the cave entrances and frogmarched down a high but narrow tunnel. They noticed that firebrand torches, fixed to the walls, gave ample light.

Jimmy had recovered some of his bravado. He addressed the Rathing apparently in charge of the escort. "Look, mate," he said, staring up at the tall creature and trying to sound casual, although his knees were shaking like jelly. "I've nothing to do with this lot. I was only trying to stop 'em from coming on to your land, like," he lied.

"You're a bigger scumbag than I thought," Bill swore angrily at Jimmy.

The Rathing didn't answer Jimmy. The party had stopped at a heavy oak door with a grill opening at

Rathing eye level. "Empty your pockets. You will give us your belongings," he ordered. The children duly obeyed, their hands trembling as they handed over their few possessions. "And those," the Rathing said, pointing to their watches. Another Rathing guard collected the belongings and placed them in a sack.

The Rathing in charge took a bunch of keys that hung on the wall and opened the cell door. "Your home," he smiled. "Temporary, of course, until we can find more fitting quarters for you."

The three lads were pushed into the cell and the door locked behind them.

The cell had been hewn out of the rock face. It was small and cold and damp. Drops of moisture clung to the stone wall. Fresh, dry straw was spread on the floor. Jack noted the few unlit candles in metal holders fixed to the wall. A small opening at ceiling height allowed a narrow shaft of sunlight to penetrate the gloom. There was no furniture.

Bill pushed Jack in his wheelchair towards the shaft of sunlight and then joined Jimmy, where both boys sat with their backs against the damp cave wall.

Jimmy whined at Jack. "I did warn you not to go through that ruddy cave. But you wouldn't ruddy well listen, would you, Mr Smarty-pants know-it-all?"

"Oh, shut up for heaven's sake," Bill said angrily. "You're just one big moan,"

"OK. What are we going to do then?" Jimmy scratched his close-shaven head. "Nothin', I suppose."

"Exactly. There's nothing we *can* do," Jack replied. "We'll just have to wait and see what these creatures have in mind for us."

"Well, they've got your mobile, Cripple," Jimmy

said to Jack. "So we can't even call for 'elp." Jimmy shrugged. "We've really 'ad it now. Unless your Indian friend thinks of using his mobile."

"Ashok doesn't have one," Jack replied.

"Well, that's great. That's really great. That's it then!" Jimmy gave a deep sigh of resignation, shrugged again and crossed his arms over his chest. They all remained silent for a while.

"Those heads stuck on poles were horrible!" Bill frowned and run his fingers nervously through his mop of blond hair. "I've never heard of the Rathings doing that."

"Perhaps that's why they want to keep everybody off this part of the beach. So nobody finds out about how they execute people," Jack remarked, then added, "And I've never heard of them using kids as slave labour."

"D'you think this particular lot of Rathings are cannibals?" Bill's eyes were wide with fright. "I mean, they're not like the Rathings we come across in the village. This lot are really nasty." He began to chew at his fingernails as he usually did when troubled about anything.

"Cannibals only eat the same kind as themselves," Jack reminded Bill.

"Rats sometimes eat humans," Jimmy mumbled uneasily. "I read it somewhere."

"Well, you'll be able to find out for yourself instead of from a book," Bill snapped, secretly pleased to see Jimmy become more agitated.

"Shut your face, slimeball," Jimmy retorted angrily. "If they're going to start on anyone they'll start on someone with the most meat on 'em." Jimmy looked at Bill pointedly and nodded. "'Morning, Fat Boy."

28

Bill didn't reply and Jack felt sorry for him. "That's not nice, Jimmy," Jack said. "Bill can't help being like he is. He's just a different build to you or me."

Jimmy patted Bill annoyingly on the shoulder. "You eat too much, mate, that's your problem."

Bill quickly changed the subject. "You got any ideas on how to get us out of this situation, Jack?"

Jack shook his head.

"Can't you have a word with that Vadek creature? Tell him we're really sorry and didn't mean to mess up his day. You've got a persuasive way of explaining things."

Jack was frightened enough about their perilous situation and he now felt an intense anger building up. "Why do you all expect me to always sort things out?" he said in an exasperated voice. "Why can't you get off my case?"

Jimmy sniggered. "Do your pals think of you as some kind of genius then, Cripple? Sitting there on your throne like some brainy professor?"

Jack ignored Jimmy's trite comment and quietly simmered in a sea of anger and frustration; anger at the group finding themselves in this situation and in knowing that even if he could find a way out of their predicament his efforts might be frustrated by his disability. He was suddenly very homesick. He knew his mum and dad loved him a lot, but because of their jobs they didn't always spend as much time with him as he would have liked. His dad was a busy solicitor and his mum was a medical consultant at a major hospital so they were always late home. He had no brothers or sisters, his only close pals being Ashok and Bill. When not playing with them, he spent his solitary hours studying or reading. He had also learned to play the piano. The years of practice and hard graft had paid off and now when he played he stroked each piano key with a deep intensity of feeling, though it was the lightness and refinement of his playing that enthralled listeners. At times of stress Jack enjoyed playing the piano. He wished he could be playing the piano now, looking out of the large bay windows onto the rolling lawns of his garden. Playing music seemed to set him free, free to soar beyond the confines of his everyday existence.

Eventually his thoughts turned to Ashok. "I hope Ashok is OK," he said anxiously.

6

The page on the calendar pinned to the wall behind Federus's desk showed the year as 2070 and the month as August.

Federus revelled in his role as Supreme Leader of the Rathings' Council. He never failed to remind others of his privileged position and that he was the second most important Rathing in the land after the President. His puffed-up, self-important demeanour was evident from the way he spoke and behaved.

He was holding his weekly meeting with the other members of the Council in his spacious office at Cheddar. At one time, long before the Rathings over-ran the country and assumed power, the building had belonged to a wealthy human.

Oil paintings of two past Rathing Presidents took pride of place on the pale pistachio-coloured walls. These had been specially commissioned and painted by the famous British painter of the time, Walter Skettle, R.A. Several large tapestries decorated the other walls and a large Persian carpet covered most of the parquet floor. A huge rectangular oak table with several oak chairs around it stood in the centre of the room. Federus sat at the head of the table, flanked by the other Council members who were seated on both sides.

The agenda item they had been discussing covered censorship of all information disseminated by the human news and entertainment media. Councillor Cerebus, in charge of Censorship, had brought to the notice of the committee the case of the editor of the *Daily Messenger* whose paper had carried an article critical of the Rathings' use of human slave labour. Councillor Cerebus was pleased to report that the editor had been executed and that the new human who had replaced him was well aware of the consequences of any repetition of such seditious material.

Councillor Laglan, in charge of Procurement, then spoke of the critical shortage of certain materials due to the blockade imposed on the British Isles. "The lack of raw materials for the pharmaceutical industry is of particular concern," he said. "We have already suffered by shortages in the automotive, engineering and catering industries, and this latest crisis is worrying. Supreme Leader Federus, I cannot stress how important it is that the Glorious President's efforts for our integration into the international community is successfully achieved as soon as possible. Time is critical. Our economy is beginning to crumble. We cannot continue to be viable if kept in isolation."

Federus nodded understandingly. "I sympathise with what you say, Laglan, and I share your concern. We must be patient. We have to remain confident that whatever the outside world hopes to achieve by starving us of essential imports, we can convince them that our inclusion on peaceful terms can only be beneficial." He paused for a few moments then announced for the first time one of the essential strategic points that President Axel had adopted in his negotiations. "We have given the humans an ultimatum. They either agree to lift the blockade and allow our Rathing nation to become part of the worldwide community or they face the risk of our invading the lands across the English Channel. The choice is theirs whether they accept us as friends or as aggressors. Our military force is ready to invade France and spread across Europe." He turned to a black-furred, heavily-built delegate who sat next to him. "Is that not so, General?"

General Zorax, Supreme Commander of the Rathing army, nodded. "We are ready for the order, Supreme Leader," he said.

"So," Federus said, "please be patient. We are making good progress. Imports will start to flow one way or the other. By co-operation or by force. Your procurement problems will soon be over, Laglan."

Federus then looked down at the papers that lay before him. "The last item on the agenda is in your court, Councillor Bardur."

Bardur, responsible for Internal Affairs, spoke. "I am pleased to say that internal matters run smoothly. The Overlords in each county report no untoward problems with the human population. And the Consuls in every village, town and city despatch similar news to their Overlords. I am pleased to say that all is well."

"I don't think it is quite true to say all is well," Federus said.

"Forgive me, Supreme Leader, have I overlooked anything?"

"You have said nothing about the troubles in one part of Cornwall."

"Overlord Vadek's province?" Bardur raised an eyebrow.

Federus nodded. "Vadek's province. The county of

Cornwall appears to be trouble-free with the exception of events taking place at Rumrunner Cove. I have heard that Vadek is having problems there with the Magars. No other Overlords have disagreements with the Magars in their counties. Why is it happening in one part of Cornwall, at Rumrunner Cove, to be precise?"

The other Rathing shrugged. "Ah, a mere domestic squabble. Too unimportant, I thought, to trouble you with. Vadek enforces the law quite rigorously. There is never any trouble from the humans. His county has the highest record of executions of humans at the drowning posts."

Federus scowled. "And of Magars. I also hear that several dozens of Magars have been executed as a result of this mere domestic squabble, as you put it. I need hardly remind you that Rathings and Magars throughout this land co-exist with a nodding respect towards each other. Why is it not so at Rumrunner Cove? It is our birthplace, and Vadek is very fortunate to have been permitted to station himself there. He should, if anything, be even more aware of his responsibilities."

"Forgive me, Supreme Leader, for not having mentioned this," Bardur mumbled.

Federus shook his head. "I cannot understand why he was ever allowed to use Rumrunner Cove as his quarters. He could reside in any of the other vast number of caves that exist in Cornwall, together with all tribe members. Rumrunner Cove should be preserved as a national monument to our heritage. And Vadek should spend more time at his office in the nearby town where his administration people work. There is a distinct lack of hands-on management by our friend."

"Oh, I am told he visits his offices once a week."

"Far too infrequent." Federus shook his head.

"And I understand that our second President, Orbal, was his uncle," Bardur explained. "Apparently he agreed to Overlord Vadek's request to station himself at Rumrunner Cove."

"Well, President Orbal is long dead. Perhaps we should consider making some changes as regards Rumrunner Cove's future status. Anyway, I want to hear at our next week's meeting that Vadek has resolved his problems with the Magars. Attend to it immediately and be sure to inform him that if he fails we shall remove him from office and assign him as a foot soldier in one of our remote centres, possibly London."

"I shall see to it," Bardur bowed his head towards Federus.

"There are also other areas of concern. The loss of Shibboleth from its hallowed place in the Temple, the use of Time Gates – the list is endless. You have also failed to mention what progress is being made against the rebels who style themselves freedom fighters. Interestingly, this problem, along with the others, exists only at Rumrunner Cove."

"The human rebels are proving to be more difficult to stop than we first thought."

"What is their leader called? Remind me again."

"Harry Carter. I'm afraid that he and his band of human renegades continue to blow up our cave entrances with dynamite and then run away to hide in caves that are too small for us to enter in pursuit. They never stay in one place, so it is difficult to pin them down."

"Then catch them in the open."

"Vadek's troops have tried."

Federus shook his head and finished Bardur's sentence: "And failed!" Then he went on: "Bardur, I have other very heavy and important matters to deal with. You know all too well how vital it is that we Rathings are accepted into the worldwide community. Once we are allowed to travel abroad we can begin the start of our clandestine plans for expansion in other countries. Our glorious President does not see why the Rathing nation should be confined to this island. It is our intention that, in time, we will assume dominance throughout the world. I am in continuous discussions with our glorious President on this issue and other vital matters of state. I really do not want to be troubled with problems that exist in one of our small communities. Is it possible that Vadek has perhaps lost his ability to maintain proper control? I suggest that the Supreme Council send a delegate to warn him of the danger he faces."

"I shall arrange this. The assigned representative will leave today."

"That is good." Federus smiled.

There was a gentle knock on the door and an elderly man entered and bowed to the assembled Rathings. He held a sheaf of papers under one arm and a notebook in his other hand.

"Excuse me, Supreme Leader," the man said. "I have the papers you asked for."

"Ah, come in, Jones," Federus beckoned the man further into the room. "Thank you." Federus then turned to the other members of the Supreme Council and said, "Some of you may not know Jones. He has been seconded from our Durham offices to take over as Chief Clerk."

Some of the Rathings gave him a perfunctory nod of acknowledgement. Others did not react.

The man placed the papers in front of Federus, bowed again, and left the room.

"I think we can now conclude our meeting, unless any of you have other matters to raise?"

All the members of the Supreme Council shook their heads. Bardur inclined his head again. "No, Supreme Leader. I think we have covered everything."

The delegates trooped out of the chamber, Bardur smarting at the indignity of having been found less than efficient in his reporting.

Federus locked the drawers of his desk, turned off the desk lamp and shuffled papers into a black leather briefcase. He was looking forward to going home. He hated time spent in buildings, although he realised this was necessary. The Secretariat was also located here. This was where those humans who were responsible for all administration matters worked. He knew that the head of the human police force, the Chief Constable, who was answerable to the Rathing Commissioner of Police, would still be working in his office further along the corridor, as would the Heads of the Utility Services, such as gas and electricity, public transport, and finance. Human civil servants worked a far longer day than their Rathing masters. Federus also longed to get home because, like other Rathings, he hated having to wear clothes, as he preferred the feel of the air on his fur, and his tunic would be quickly shed once indoors. He also yearned for the comfort of home, located in one of the vast caves with its numerous cells in the exclusive Rathing suburb at Cheddar Gorge. His cave home was so much more comfortable and cooler than the claustrophobic atmosphere of enclosed human buildings.

On his way out, he looked in at his secretary. She was a young woman and was sitting at her computer typing emails. "Good night, Sarah," he said. "Don't forget I need the analysis of those figures for tomorrow."

She looked up from her work. "Good night, Supreme Leader. And you will remember that you have a meeting with the President at eight tomorrow."

He nodded. "Yes, thank you. Jones has already given me the documents." With that, he turned and walked down the corridor, a satisfied smile on his face.

7

The Magar dropped Ashok gently on the cliff-top plateau. The others placed the old man in a nest of twigs filled with feathers and gathered anxiously around him. Some of them began tending to his wound.

Ashok sat against a rock, his teeth chattering through fright. He looked around the cliff top. Hundreds of these odd-looking half-bird half-human creatures dotted the area. There were also numerous domed nests that looked like they were made of loosely woven sticks. He noticed clumps of mud and grass spilling over the nest cup on some. Several of the creatures were nesting in them.

He was not only afraid for himself, but also concerned at what had happened to his friends. He reckoned that Jack and Jimmy would possibly handle the situation and keep cool heads. He'd always recognised that Jack was a very strong character and had an inbuilt resilience despite his incapacity. Jimmy was a tough nut and would no doubt give as good as he got. He wasn't so sure about Bill, though. Bill tended to be defeatist at the best of times, and panic if things weren't going right. He doubted if Bill could cut it. Ashok had always thought it might be because Bill's gran tended to mollycoddle and fuss over him all the time. Ashok and Jack liked Bill because of his kind nature, although he had a tendency to complain and sulk if things weren't going his way. In some ways, Ashok wished he could be with them.

When things had quietened down and the Magars had moved away from the man, Ashok walked over and sat besides him.

"How's the wound?" he asked.

"Not too bad, thanks. Could have been worse."

Ashok had been puzzled at the apparent animosity that existed between the two sets of clones. "How come these Magars came to our aid? They seemed to really hate the Rathings down there."

"There's not much love lost between them," the old man replied. "The reason why they snatched us from the Rathings was only to annoy them. Not necessarily because of any fondness for us."

Ashok shrugged. "As they're both types of clone I'd have thought they'd get on with each other."

"I believe they do in the rest of the country. But there's a kind of vendetta going on here. I've seen it several times."

"Sorry? How come? You mean you've been here before?"

The man nodded. "I was press-ganged into the labour force several years ago. I've been here for a long time."

"Wow!" Ashok exclaimed. "You mean you're a slave?"

The man nodded.

"What's a matter with your eyes?"

The man placed a hand against his side and gave a slight moan of pain.

"You OK?" Ashok asked anxiously.

The man nodded. "I was sentenced to death for talking in front of a Rathing. They took my eyes out before tying me to a drowning post."

Ashok shook his head. "Gruesome! What's a drowning post?" he asked.

The man smiled. "Something I hope you never experience. A drowning post is where they put a condemned person to drown at high tide". He then asked, "What were you and your friends doing on the beach?"

"We came through for a lark."

"Foolish. And dangerous. You young people should have your heads tested. You don't do things for a lark where Rathings are concerned."

"What'll happen to my friends?" Ashok asked.

"I really don't know. Vadek – that's the Rathing leader down there – might let them go. And then on the other hand, he might put them with the slaves. But he's never taken kids as slaves, so on balance I think he might give them a ticking-off and let them return through the cave."

"And what about us? D'you think these Magars might let us go?"

"I hope so. Magars are quite docile by nature, apart from their scraps with the Rathings, so they'll probably take us down to the beach later."

Ashok leant back against the rock face. He now wished that he hadn't got carried away with his adventurous enthusiasm and travelled through the cave. But Jack seemed so happy at doing something daring that the spirit of the moment had clouded all reasonable thinking. He turned to the man. "Taking your eyes out seems a bit ruthless."

"That's the punishment in store before drowning for any slave who breaks the Rathings' law."

The old man stopped as a fit of coughing overcame him. Ashok was concerned to note a trickle of blood spill from the man's mouth. He didn't know what he could do to ease the man's obvious pain.

"Look," he said, "you're coughing blood."

"I'm all right. I'm all right," the man croaked and gave another painful moan.

Ashok didn't like the fact that the man was coughing blood. "I reckon you're more injured than you think. Shall I ask these Magars if they've got anything to ease your pain?"

The man gave a weak laugh. "I don't think they go in for stocks of painkillers. Don't worry, son, I'll be OK. I think I'd better rest now." He felt around until he found Ashok's hand. He patted it gently. "We'll talk later, if you don't mind."

But Ashok was still curious. "If you were tied to this drowning post you mention, how come you were on the beach hiding behind the rocks?"

"Some Magars flew down and untied me. To annoy the Rathings, I think. They left me on the beach. I was hoping to go through the cave to Rumrunner Beach."

"I guess we spoilt it for you. Our turning up like that. Sorry."

The old man shrugged. "It's no matter. I doubt I could have made it without any sight."

Ashok looked at the side of the man's chest and noted whitish-pink blood seeping from it. The man suddenly began to groan more loudly and toss his head in extreme pain. He went into yet another fit of coughing and this time the blood from his mouth was more than a trickle.

Ashok felt totally helpless, not knowing what to do to stem the flow of blood. He took a rather grubby handkerchief from his pocket and handed it to the man, who wiped his mouth with it. "Thanks, my boy. I'm going to try and get some sleep now. Hopefully it'll help the pain die down."

8

Vadek had called a meeting of senior Rathings. Seated around a circular table were Vadek and to his left a tiny, wizened old Rathing who had lost most of the fur on his head except for a few wisps that were long and white and flopped around his tiny ears. The fur on his chin had also turned white, giving the impression of a beard. This was Panuf, the High Priest and Keeper of the Scrolls. To Panuf's left sat a very big Rathing wearing an eyepatch. He was General Garbath, Military Commander of the Rathing army in Cornwall and Vadek's younger brother.

Garbath cast his one good eye over the other delegates in attendance. They were all, of course, well known to him but he held little regard for any of them, with the possible exception of Superintendent Dalus. Dalus commanded the body of guards who oversaw the building and tunnelling operations carried out by the slave workforce. Garbath recognised that Dalus was a highly competent executive, but sometimes felt that his harsh treatment of the human slaves could be toned down. Dalus, short and burly, sat beetle-browed, chomping at the bit, anxious to be finished with the inevitable lengthy discussions that always took place at these meetings; he was keen to get back to supervising his work in the caves. Captain Sarum was seated next to Garbath. Sarum always had problems with his breathing. Garbath avoided turning his gaze towards Sarum. He could hear the constant sniffle, as if Sarum had a cold or a blocked nose, and was aware that Sarum had begun to explore his nostrils with a long fingernail. Sarum and his officers were in charge of supervising public order amongst the Rathing tribe and ensuring that all edicts issued by the Supreme Council at Cheddar were carried out.

No Rathing would be considered as having a kindly nature, but the one who lounged next to Dalus was a particularly nasty-looking creature. One side of his face was crushed and badly scarred, causing the eye to be pushed far down towards his cheek. This was a legacy of a Magar having stamped hard on him as he lay on the ground badly hurt in battle. He was Commissioner Batanguma and was responsible for controlling the food and materials stores and for advising Vadek when replenishments were needed. Garbath disliked Batanguma intensely.

But what particularly intrigued General Garbath was the presence of the Rathing who had been accorded the special place on Vadek's right side. Garbath studied the visitor with interest. It was very unusual for a delegate from the Supreme Council to make a sudden visit. Whatever reason had prompted his attendance must have been important. Darma was an officious-looking character, small and tubby and, unusually for a Rathing, had a pair of rimless spectacles balanced on the end of his long rat nose.

Vadek wore an old-fashioned policeman's helmet. He had to tie it with a ribbon around his chin as it was several sizes too small for his enormous skull. He was very particular as to what colour ribbon he used, depending on the occasion. He invariably took hours trying several coloured ribbons before settling on the one that he felt to be most appropriate. Vanity was one of Vadek's many questionable traits. Today it was a green one. Vadek always wore his policeman's helmet either at important meetings or in major battles with the Magars. He believed it gave him an air of importance.

All those seated around the table represented the elite of the tribe.

Vadek looked at the assembled audience. He chose his words carefully as he addressed them. "We firstly wish to extend warm, fraternal greetings to our distinguished visitor from head office. I am delighted to present to you Councillor Darma of the Supreme Council."

The chamber thundered with the sound of giant paws thumping the table in formal salutations.

Vadek then turned to Darma. "I believe, Councillor, that there is a specific reason for your visit. Do you wish to enlighten us?"

Darma studied the assembled delegates over the rim of his spectacles. He said nothing for quite some time. The others began to fidget in their seats. At last he spoke, his voice light, oily and disdainful. "I have instructions direct from Supreme Leader Federus to address you on the concerns that the Supreme Council have in respect of the situation existing here at Rumrunner Cove.

"We do not know what the reasons are for the antagonism that exists between you and the Magars, but this state of affairs must be resolved without delay. It is true that we Rathings have little regard for Magars, who share neither our faith nor our ambitions. Nevertheless, Rathing and Magar co-exist

46

on non-belligerent terms throughout Britain and we wish to see the same apply here. You, as Rathings and therefore the more superior and intelligent race, must make a determined effort to achieve a peaceful co-existence. Find out what bothers the Magars and give them what they want – within reason, of course. In other words, make peace with them.

"We are also troubled by the fact that you have allowed Shibboleth to be stolen from the Temple. Shibboleth is the formula of our creation. It was bequeathed to us by our god, Professor Andersen, who created us." He turned and looked at Panuf. "You are the High Priest and Keeper of the Scrolls, are you not?"

Panuf nodded, his chest puffed out with pride at being recognised.

"In your exalted position it is your ultimate responsibility to guard Shibboleth. You appear to have failed in your duty."

Panuf's pride deserted him, scuttling away in shame and fear.

"As you know," Darma continued, "the original Shibboleth is held at our headquarters at Cheddar. Copies are with all Overlords and none have gone missing with the exception of yours. It is important that Shibboleth is displayed in every temple in the land and we cannot tolerate the fact that none exists here. Your priority is to ensure the return of Shibboleth. You will correct this situation immediately." Darma paused and then asked Vadek a direct question. "Would you like us to send some of our elite troops to retrieve Shibboleth for you?"

"No, no. Thank you, Councillor, but we can manage," he replied.

"I hope more efficiently than so far." For the first

time since his arrival, Darma smiled. "I can well understand your reluctance to accept assistance."

Garbath smiled to himself. Of course Vadek would be reluctant to accept help. That was the last thing Vadek wanted. It would mean admitting defeat. It would mean he was not capable of properly managing affairs.

Darma then continued. "The other matter that worries us is your apparent inability to crush the band of human rebels who call themselves freedom fighters. Frankly, we are at a loss to understand why you have not managed this."

"May I say something?" Vadek asked.

Darma shook his head. "I'm afraid not. I did not come here to hold discussions. I am here to tell you what the Supreme Council wishes to see done. You may have as many debates as you feel necessary amongst yourselves. The main purpose . . ."

Garbath interrupted the Councillor. "Councillor. This is my responsibility. I strongly object to your making sweeping statements and not allowing a response. It is a well-known and established fact that catching insurgents is a time-consuming task. You may say that you are at a loss to understand why we have not succeeded. I invite you to spend some days with me and my troops on patrol. You may learn something about the difficulties experienced when hunting down saboteurs."

Darma smiled. "You speak bluntly, like a soldier. However, I repeat, I am not here to hold discussions. It is my brief to advise your Overlord of the concerns of the Supreme Council. I am quite sure that there are explanations for every one of the problems. The Supreme Council do not want explanations. They want results."

Garbath scowled and sat back in his chair, his arms folded across his massive chest.

"And finally, it is our understanding that there have been recent incidents where recalcitrant Rathings have been punished by being sent through a Time Gate. This is in direct contravention of laid-down edicts. This must stop immediately." Darma removed his glasses and gave them a quick polish before replacing them very carefully on his nose.

Vadek had lost his usual haughty manner. He was unused to criticism and he felt uncomfortable. He adjusted his policeman's helmet that had slipped over his brow and looked nervously at Darma. This was bad news. He had never imagined that his favourite form of punishment administered against a disobedient Rathing would have reached the ears of his superiors. There had been only a few such sentences passed and they had been carried out in secret by a handful of trusted confidants. He felt weak at the knees.

Darma rose. "Overlord Vadek. I now wish to speak with you alone. You may continue with your meeting afterwards."

Vadek also got up from his chair. "Of course, of course, Councillor. Perhaps we can adjourn to my private quarters?"

Darma nodded. He then turned to the other seated delegates. "Heed my words. The Supreme Council do not send a Councillor such as me to outlying posts unless there are serious matters that concern us. Vadek here may be your superior, but you are all responsible." With that, he turned and followed Vadek from the room.

Vadek's nervousness was evident in the way he fussed around making sure that Darma was seated in the most comfortable chair and was offered some refreshment, which Darma declined.

"Vadek," Darma said, "forgive me if I appeared curt in refusing to discuss matters at the meeting. What I have to say is for your ears only."

Vadek nodded. "Of course, of course, Councillor. I fully understand."

"It is important, vital for you personally, that you sort out the problems here. Supreme Leader Federus is most unhappy and your position as Overlord has a big question mark hanging over it. We are particularly annoyed to learn of your total disregard of Supreme Council orders pertaining to Time Gates. What arrogance on your part gives you the right to think you can use the Time Gates as a form of punishment in direct contravention of orders?"

Vadek gave a nervous gulp. "It was . . ." He heard his words come out in a high, nervous squeak. He cleared his throat and began again. "Er, it happened on a few occasions only. To act as a deterrent."

Darma shook his head. "You know all too well that Time Gates project the subject into the past. A Rathing found wandering about in a land many decades before now, when we did not exist, would cause alarm and also, more seriously, raise questions amongst the human population. He could be killed or captured. The humans of that time would interrogate a captured Rathing. I accept that we Rathings can endure great pain but we do not know what methods may be employed to gain information. Do you see the seriousness of it?"

Vadek nodded. He was so nervous that he did not dare allow himself to speak. Another squeak from his mouth would be embarrassing.

Darma continued in his oily manner. "It is true that

50

we discovered Time Gates only recently, but if humans establish the location of a Time Gate there is nothing to say they might not decide to find out more by using a reverse Time Gate. Time Gates are not one-way streets. They can handle two-way traffic. We do not wish to have unwelcome visitors from the past. Do you understand?"

Darma studied Vadek over the rim of his glasses. He seemed to be waiting for an answer. Vadek had to say something this time. He cleared his throat several times before speaking.

"I fully understand, Councillor. You have my assurance that this will not happen again."

Darma nodded. "It is what we will expect of you. Finally, I must tell you that Supreme Leader Federus has instructed me to tell you the following. I repeat his own words: 'Be sure to inform him that if he fails we shall remove him from office and assign him as a foot soldier in one of our remote areas, possibly London.'"

This was shattering news for Vadek. To lose the confidence of the Supreme Council and, more importantly, the Supreme Leader himself was alarming. To be reduced to the ranks and transferred to a remote location such as London was a death sentence. London, without any natural network of caves, obliged Rathings located there to live in humans' houses and deprived them of the comforts of cave dwelling. Vadek could not have found himself facing a worse situation. Things looked bad. Very bad.

Then Darma cast him a lifeline. "I now have something of great importance to tell you. What I am about to say is for your ears only. When you have heard my news, you will be the only other person in the country to know about it other than our Glorious President, Supreme Leader Federus and me. At this stage, there is nothing in writing."

Vardek nodded and tried very hard to assume a confidential, trustworthy and understanding air. "I am honoured, Councillor."

"What has been concluded by our Glorious President, and discussed with Supreme Leader Federus, is that we are not happy about the uncontrolled breeding among humans. It has been decided, therefore, that other than those humans who hold positions of responsibility under our rule and who contribute to society, the remainder of the human population will be told that they must not produce more than one offspring. Those who disobey will be imprisoned and their child placed in our slave-labour centres for eventual assignment, at the right age, to work in the caves and other areas where such labour is required."

"Controlled human breeding!" Vadek exclaimed under his breath.

"We have agreed for the pilot scheme to begin here, where we first originated. It will be your responsibility to introduce this in Cornwall. You will run the programme, monitor households and the number of births per household, carry out punishment for those who disobey and submit statistics to headquarters. If all goes smoothly under your control, this scheme will be introduced throughout the country. Any failure on your part will mean your instant removal from office and another Overlord appointed to carry out our instructions. However, as negotiations with the UN and the USA are still at a delicate stage, we will not launch this project until after we have been granted a seat in the United

52

Nations and when all embargoes against us are lifted."

Vadek grinned. "This is most exciting news, Councillor."

"You may discuss this only when you are told you may do so and only with a few of your most trusted colleagues – those who will be responsible, under your command, for carrying out our programme. And I stress, do not make this decision known until you are told you may do so.

"Ensure that the pilot scheme here works well and you will find that the shadow that hangs over you at present will vanish and honours be heaped upon you. Succeed and a seat awaits you in the Supreme Council. So, I urge you that in the meantime you resolve your current problems as quickly as possible. Is that understood?"

"Without any doubt, Councillor. And may I say that I am grateful to you." A seat on the Supreme Council! Vadek felt a tremor of excitement course through his veins.

Darma nodded and rose from his seat. As he made his way out, he turned to Vadek and pointed at the helmet. "Tell me, Vadek, why do you wear that ridiculous hat?"

9

Vadek returned to the main conference chamber where the others had remained. They stood in small groups, discussing the way the meeting had gone and Darma's statement of the Supreme Council's disquiet at the state of affairs at Rumrunner Cove.

Vadek tried very hard to put on a brave face as he sat down. Needless to say, he would not tell any of them what Darma had said in the privacy of Vadek's private chamber.

"We have heard what Councillor Darma had to say. Obviously, we must take immediate action. Before we discuss making peace with the Magars, we must find some solution as to how we can retrieve Shibboleth from them. As the Councillor said, it is a priority."

Captain Sarum leant forward, his forearms resting on the table. He was tall and thin with reddish fur.

"It will be difficult to retrieve Shibboleth – *sniff* – unless we can get the Magars to agree to give it back – *sniff* – so that it is here in its rightful place – *sniff* – in our Temple and amongst us. *Sniff.*" He began to pick his nose again.

The others nodded their heads in agreement, except for General Garbath.

"You state the obvious, Sarum," Garbath snorted.

54

"The Magars have Shibboleth and we are unable to retrieve it. You all know that despite numerous attempts by my troops, we are far too big to scale the cliff and get Shibboleth back. Why, you will remember that we even built wooden towers and dragged them to the cliff face in the hope that our soldiers could climb inside and be protected against attack. Unfortunately, we couldn't build them tall enough to reach the cliff top without them toppling over. We might as well accept that, short of a miracle, we can say goodbye to Shibboleth."

"A somewhat defeatist attitude if I may say so," Vadek intervened, raising his eyebrows in seeming surprise. "As military commander you would surely not allow one setback to deter you from exploring other methods?" Although he had never voiced this, Vadek was of the opinion that Garbath was largely to blame for Shibboleth not having been retrieved. After all, Vadek thought, it was the responsibility of the military to resolve the problem.

"If you were prepared to accept the assistance offered by that Councillor fellow, helicopters flown by human pilots with an elite military force of Rathings on board could easily storm the cliff plateau and get hold of Shibboleth," Garbath stated bluntly. "We do not have the proper resources here to deal with this."

Vadek shook his head. "No. It is a local matter for us to resolve. I do not want interference of any kind, whether in the form of assistance or otherwise."

There was a distinct coldness, an underlying tension, between the brothers. The two had never got along, even in childhood, and their animosity had grown over the years. Garbath was blind in his left eye, over which he wore a black eyepatch, and a little deaf in his left ear; his injuries were sustained during a very hard-fought battle with the Magars. When he did not particularly want to see or hear anything, or pretend so, he turned his left side to the speaker. Such a delaying tactic helped give him time to consider an appropriate response.

He used this ploy now.

He glared at Vadek. He spoke with the same culti-vated accent as Vadek but without any of the arro-gance or seeming condescension. "I have some ideas. But tell me, brother, as Overlord, how do *you* propose to get the Magar's agreement to return it?"

"That is what we are to discuss," Vadek said patiently. He was still too shocked at being taken to task by Darma for his normally arrogant manner to make itself evident.

"I think I have the answer," Panuf said.

He paused, as if deliberately waiting for his words to register with the others.

Vadek felt very much stressed. He really didn't want this meeting to go round in circles, discussing everything and agreeing to nothing. He nodded impatiently. "Yes, yes, do go on, Panuf."

Panuf smiled. "General Garbath is quite correct when he says that our soldiers are too big to scale the cliff but we now have in our midst some human children found on our beach. Why not use them?"

The others muttered amongst themselves, shak-ing their heads in puzzlement. They could not quite see what the recently captured human children had in common with the loss of Shibboleth or its return.

"Interestingly, it seems the Magars have adopted a new tactic to annoy us," Panuf continued. "In the past, prisoners condemned to death were left to meet their fate. Obviously, we never tied captured

56

Magars to the drowning posts as their compatriots would have rescued them. But humans and Droon prisoners? They were left to drown, as is the custom. But now the Magars seem to have found a new way to irritate us. They rescued a condemned prisoner, as witnessed by them saving the man whom we tied to the drowning post the other day."

Vadek tapped his right paw impatiently on the table. "Get to the point, Panuf."

"My point is this. Why don't we get the human children to steal Shibboleth from the Magars? *They* are small."

"And how do you propose doing that? *Sniff*," Captain Sarum asked with an amused smile playing about his thin lips. "Is it your intention to tie the humans – *sniff* – to the drowning posts so that the Magars save them? *Sniff*." The investigation of his nostrils continued, this time with even greater enthusiasm.

"No, no. If we did that we would have to take their eyes out and that would defeat the whole purpose. And not to blind them would cause suspicion amongst the Magar. No, my plan is simple. We tell the human children that we propose to infiltrate them into the Magar encampment with the sole purpose that they bring back Shibboleth. In return for their undertaking this task, we shall promise to release them from slave labour and allow them to return to their homes. The only feasible way is for two of them to make a, so-called, escape from the workforce when they bathe in the sea after work in the tunnels. The guards will be told to pretend that they haven't seen the escape. The other boy will be held as hostage. I am confident that the Magars will rescue those on the beach; it will present another opportunity for them to annoy us. One I am sure they would not want to miss." Panuf raised an index finger and continued: "That is our first objective realised. This will mean that we have successfully placed two of the human children with the Magars."

Panuf raised his next finger. "Second objective. The humans will take Shibboleth when the opportunity presents itself. I am sure there will be many such instances. The Magars do not guard Shibboleth. They simply leave it stuck on an outcrop, ignored and neglected. The humans can return via the narrow ledge. If this proves awkward, they can throw the canister containing Shibboleth onto the beach, where we can quickly collect it."

A third stubby little finger joined its cousins looking skywards. "Third. We will make it clear to the children that if they tell the Magars the real purpose of their assignment, their remaining friend held hostage will be put to death. Humans are as bad as Magars for their tendency to show consideration towards others. They would not let their companion be executed. So they would say nothing to the Magars."

The assembled delegates began talking excitedly amongst themselves. They appeared to like the idea.

"Do you really think the Magars won't suspect a set-up?" Superintendent Dalus asked.

"Not if everyone plays their part properly. But if it is unsuccessful, we must accept that we tried our best. We will have to devise another plan, that's all. Success inevitably acknowledges he who is patient." Panuf then turned to Vadek and continued, "May I respectfully advance a further suggestion?"

"Go on," Vadek commanded. "But any agreed strategy to retrieve Shibboleth must succeed at the first attempt. We do not have the luxury of time to try different things. Nor the comfort of patience. I really do not want to experience another visit from Councillor Darma."

"I have every confidence my idea will work," Panuf said. "My further suggestion is that I would like to propose that in order to facilitate the children in their return journey we create a diversion further away from the cliff path. Perhaps some of our troops can go to the other end of the cliffs and throw spears or fire their guns at the Magars. This will distract their attention from the children."

"Very good. We shall do that. As regards the children, there are only two of them able to do what you propose. The third one is confined to a wheelchair."

Panuf continued. "Precisely. The boy who sits in his contraption would be of no use. I am not sure how the bigger, older boy, the one with the hard face and shaven head, would handle the situation as I suspect he is cowardly by nature and may panic. But he will be forced to carry out the assignment on pain of torture. The other, the fat boy, would obey without argument."

"Your idea is sound, Panuf. As is usual, I shall see them first and will then pass them on to you."

"I shall instruct them to undertake this mission and will point out the penalty for failure."

As the assembled Rathings made their way out, Panuf leant close to Vadek and whispered, "May I have a further quiet word with you alone?"

Vadek nodded.

Panuf waited until the others had left the chamber. "I don't think our problems are made any easier, Overlord, by your brother's recent behaviour. He has a strong following of admirers and I suspect that he is planning to, er . . ." Panuf hesitated.

Vadek waited for Panuf to continue. Panuf looked distinctly ill at ease. "Well, come on, out with it," Vadek prompted.

"I don't know how to say this without possibly upsetting you."

"Try."

"Rumour has it that General Garbath may be planning to overthrow you and assume leadership as Overlord."

Vadek nodded. "I have also heard this from other quarters. I doubt the veracity of such rumours. In any case, only the Supreme Council can appoint an Overlord."

Panuf was too wily not to have missed the implications of Darma's visit. He knew that what he was now about to say needed to be carefully worded. He did not want to alienate Vadek. "Forgive me for saying this, but may I surmise that the Councillor's visit was prompted by some question about your leadership?"

Vadek said angrily, "You presume too much, Panuf."

"Forgive me again. I did not intend to presume. I only suggest that if the Supreme Council is unhappy about things taking place here, they may not be averse to a new Overlord assuming command. If your brother does take over, is it likely that they will punish him and reinstate you? It is a fact we must consider. I am, of course, very worried about such a situation arising."

Vadek gave a wry smile. "Of course you are, Panuf. If I were not Overlord you might not last long as High Priest and Keeper of the Scrolls."

"Oh Great Leader . . ." Panuf shook his head, bowed, and looked obsequiously at Vadek. "I assure you most humbly that my concern is only for you. I have no fears for myself."

Vadek raised a cynical eyebrow. "Whatever," he said. "Even though I may doubt the truth of the rumours about my brother's supposed intentions, rumours sometimes have the nasty habit of becoming reality. Rumours undermine the maintenance of good order. The important thing is that we get those young humans to retrieve Shibboleth. It is vitally important for both of us. It is important for the good of our tribe. It is important that we appease the Supreme Council."

Panuf bowed. "How right you are," he said.

10

Jack, Bill, and Jimmy had been sitting quietly, terrified at their predicament, when they heard the cell door being unlocked. A Rathing stood at the entrance. He had to bend down to look into the cell, as the ceiling was too low to allow him to enter in an upright position.

"You," he said, pointing at Jack. "Overlord Vadek wants to talk to you."

"Why me?" Jack asked nervously.

"You will come," the Rathing said angrily. "I have my orders."

"I can't move in this alone, not on rough ground. Someone must push me."

"I'll do it," Jimmy volunteered, rising quickly, anxious to leave the confines of the cell.

"OK, thanks, Jimmy," Jack said reluctantly. He would have preferred Bill to help him, but thought that Jimmy might be more useful in a tight corner. Although what either of them could do against these giants was debatable.

"Follow," the Rathing ordered.

Jimmy pushed Jack's wheelchair and followed the Rathing along brightly lit winding tunnels until they came to a heavy oak door. The Rathing opened it and stood back, gesturing them forward.

"Please enter," Vadek said. "You must be thirsty. Can I offer you some refreshment? Some water perhaps?" His whole demeanour was far more welcoming and sociable than it had been on the beach.

Jack shook his head. Jimmy said, "Yeah – unless you got a Pepsi."

Vadek clapped his paws.

He looked at Jack. "I understand you cannot walk and must sit in that vehicle. Why is that?"

"He's a cripple," Jimmy said quickly. "Got something called spina bifida."

Jack was intensely irritated by Jimmy's comment. "I am not a cripple. It's just that I am not very well," he replied.

"It is usual to stand in my presence," Vadek said.

"I can stand, but not for long," Jack explained.

"It's his legs, you see." Jimmy was trying to be helpful. "He's got no strength in them. They're a bit useless, like."

Vadek nodded. "Then I shall make an exception in your case."

A small side door opened and a middle-aged man entered. His clothes were ragged and dirty. His feet were bare. He moved slowly, like a zombie, a broken spirit, eyes cast downwards. He bowed low to Vadek and walked towards the two boys. He held two gold goblets on a tray. He did not look at either boy but remained staring at the floor.

"Drink," Vadek ordered. "Refresh yourselves. You'll find the water here very good."

The boys gulped down the ice-cold water. They then handed the goblets back to the man, who turned and went out through the small side door.

"The water is fresh from the stream that flows from the cliff tops. I trust your thirst is quenched?"

Vadek rose and walked towards the boys, his huge frame towering over them.

"It is not our practice to take children as slave labourers but your uninvited presence on our beach left us with no other option. I believe it is only common courtesy for me to explain to all newcomers what we expect from our slaves. You will convey this information to your companion."

Jack struggled to his feet and leant on the arm of his wheelchair. He felt that what he had to say would be better said whilst standing and confronting his adversary. "It would make sense for you to let us go. If we don't return home soon our families will come looking for us. And the police also."

Vadek laughed again. "Your threats are empty words. No one will come for you."

"You wanna bet?" Jimmy spat.

"No one dares question our authority. You forget that whilst we permit you humans to lead your lives as you wish, we Rathings remain the supreme rulers. However, it is possible, just possible, that you may not remain slaves for long, in return for your doing something for us."

"You mean you'll let us go back home?" Jimmy asked eagerly.

Vadek nodded. "Most certainly."

He walked around his chamber as he continued to speak to the two boys. "But let me first tell you what is expected of you. The most important rule for you to remember is that things are done differently here. In the villages, towns and cities you are allowed to converse whilst Rathings are about. We impose no restrictions on the human population. But here we need new caves or the present ones enlarged. This is why we employ slave labour. For the sake of efficiency, there is a strict rule that must be observed. A rule that you will not have come across before. Here, you will not speak to another human whilst you are in the presence of a Rathing. To do so will result in your death. You will work at whatever duties are assigned to you by Work Masters. Obey your Work Master and you will live. Upset him and you will die. Death is by drowning. You are taken to the beach and there we first gouge your eyes out and place them on the rocks next to you. It is a long-established tradition and there is a reason for this. Your eyes will see the whole cycle of your execution. You will be tied to a post on the beach and drown when the tide rises and the sea sweeps over you. Your head is then cut off and you will, of course, watch as it is stuck on a pole by the cave entrance. Your body is left to rot in one of the deepest caves with others who have shared the same fate, and your eyes will be placed next to your body so that you can witness it rot and crumble into dust. Quite a unique experience, don't you think?"

The two boys stared at each other, terrified at the vivid description of execution.

Vadek walked to the main door of his room, opened it and beckoned to someone in the outside corridor. "Panuf, if you could spare me a minute of your precious time?"

Jack and Jimmy watched a wizened Rathing enter. A long black cloak covered his scrawny shoulders and he held some kind of wand in his left paw. He was considerably smaller than Vadek, yet still towered over the two boys.

"Overlord." He bowed before Vadek and saluted him by tapping his left breast with his right paw.

"This is Panuf, our High Priest and Keeper of the

Sacred Scrolls." Then turning to Panuf Vadek said, "I leave you to persuade these young humans that the possibility of their returning to their homes is dependent on their co-operation in retrieving Shibboleth for us."

The other Rathing looked quizzically at the boys. "This one," he pointed at Jack, "why does he sit before you? Why does he not stand?"

"He has damaged legs," Vadek explained. "They are of no use to him. But I think the others regard him as their leader of sorts, perhaps supposedly because of his wheelchair and the analogy to a throne?"

Panuf said, "I see."

Jimmy snorted.

"Then, Panuf, may I leave it to you to explain to them their task? General Garbath has asked to see me again and I don't like to keep him waiting."

Panuf said with a smile, "How fortunate we are to have as our Overlord someone as wise and cautious as you." He bowed. "I shall talk with these two. It is an honour to obey your commands, as always, Overlord." He opened the door and called out to some Rathing guards. "Take these two to the Temple. I shall be there shortly."

11

Two Rathing guards appeared at the door of the small cell where Bill sat on his own. He was chewing away at his fingers. The Rathings carried lit torches and escorted him to another part of the cave labyrinth. They entered a long, winding tunnel. They turned to their right and down another tunnel. Firebrands, fixed on the right wall, lit the tunnel. To the left, a long cage housed a large group of people, men and women; a miserable, motley crowd who sat huddled against the cave walls. The sound of conversation stopped immediately the Rathings entered the tunnel.

"Welcome to your new quarters." The leading Rathing gave a short laugh, unlocked the cage door and pushed Bill in.

Bill stood by the door, frightened and unsure. The only light present was that cast by the flickering firebrands on the walls of the tunnel outside the cell. A nauseating smell, a mixture of stale air and sweat made him retch. The straw on the floor was wet and stuck to his trainers. Some of the shadowy forms began to move towards him like an advancing grey mist. The silence was suddenly broken as the shadows began eagerly to fire questions at him. They were all talking at the same time and it was difficult for Bill to make any sense of what was being said.

"Silence!" a voice barked, and the torrent of sound ceased as suddenly as it had begun. A tall, thin, elderly man with piercing blue eyes, high cheek-bones and long grey hair and beard walked towards Bill. He wore an open neck, short-sleeved off-white shirt and light-tan trousers. A pair of battered brogues completed the ensemble.

"Welcome, friend. My name's Doctor Fournier. Pierre Fournier. You must forgive this eagerness of some of the prisoners to want to speak to you, but newcomers are rare." He spoke with a heavy accent, which Bill reckoned, because of the man's name, was possibly French. The man then turned to the others. "We must not forget the shock each one of us felt when we were first brought here. Come on, *mes amis*, give this child some breathing space. Let him have time to adjust to his surroundings." The other prisoners nodded, each one feeling guilty at their enthusiasm to ask questions.

The man turned to Bill. He saw a short, fair-haired plump boy wearing a T-shirt, shorts and trainers. His dimpled knees were grazed and dirty, his chubby face smeared with grime and tear-stained. The boy looked very frightened and stood at the cell door gnawing at his fingernails.

"As I said, my name's Doctor Fournier. For my sins I happen to have been elected a spokesman of sorts for we slave labourers. I must say that it is very unusual for a child to be seized for slave labour. This is most puzzling." He put his arm around the boy's shoulders in a fatherly and protective manner. "Come, you're quite safe here. Sorry about the smell. You'll get used to it. As you may notice, there are no

68

holes or openings to allow in any fresh air. We just slowly stifle in here until we are let out to work or for our evening meal. Still, would you care to introduce yourself? Just take your time."

"I, I'm, my name's Bill," Bill stuttered nervously.

"Welcome, Bill." Fournier shook his hand warmly.

He pointed at some straw that was dry. "Come, sit and make yourself comfortable. We've just finished our tunnelling work for today and we will be going to dinner soon. We're all pretty well exhausted, but, as you can see, some have questions to ask. Most of us have been here for years so we're anxious for news of the outside world. I'm afraid that all newcomers go through an initial grilling."

12

Jack and Jimmy were escorted into a cave that was furnished like a church. Hundreds of candles lit the cavern and a number of faded tapestries decorated the rock face. They were not unlike those the boys had seen on the walls of Vadek's chamber. Old church pews were lined up, facing a huge altar at the far end. Various artefacts – what looked like Bibles, chalices, bottles, various pieces of wood and bundles of clothes – were placed on the altar. In the centre of the altar stood a wooden model of a Rathing. Its paws were designed as if it should have been holding something that was now no longer there. Fresh straw covered the floor. The atmosphere was cool, with fresh air filtering from the numerous circular holes cut into the rock ceiling.

Panuf entered. He moved towards an ornately carved throne to the side of the altar and sat on it.

"Our Overlord has ordained that you should undertake a small task. On the cliff top, in easy view, is a small gold-coloured tin. This tin contains something precious to us. That is its rightful place." He nodded towards the empty-handed model on the altar. "How the tin came to be on the cliff top is of no concern to you. Our soldiers are too big to climb up there to get it back. We wish you to bring it to us."

"Isn't that where those bird-thingies live?" Jimmy queried.

"Listen to what I have to say," Panuf snapped.

He clasped his paws across his little potbelly and explained the plan in detail. He concluded by saying, "There will be no proper escape, of course, and you will make no attempt to re-enter the cave that leads to your beach. To do so will result in your recapture and immediate execution. Guards will be posted in the cave. All you need do is try and attract the attention of the Magars so that they come down and take you to their cliff-top dwelling."

Panuf rose and walked towards the two boys. The flickering candlelight enhanced his reflection, making him appear to be several sizes larger. He spoke directly to Jimmy.

"Your friend here" – he pointed at Jack – "will remain as hostage. So that you do not spend more time with the Magars than is necessary, I asked Jago, our Chief Executioner, to devise a method to ensure you make a swift return with Shibboleth. His idea is brilliant. You" – he again pointed at Jack – "will be tied by thick rope and suspended over a pit in which sharpened wooden stakes have been placed. Jago will periodically singe the strands of rope so that they begin to fray. He is quite expert at doing this sort of thing. His timing will be impeccable to ensure that only a little bit of rope starts to fray each time it is lit. This gradually fraying of the rope will take place over a period of three days. That is your time limit in which to retrieve Shibboleth and return it to us. If you fail to complete your assignment in this time limit, the last frayed part of the rope will come apart and your friend here . . ." —Panuf smiled at Jack— ". . . will plummet down onto the sharpened wooden stakes. He will be impaled. After his death, we will cut his head off and place it with the other heads of executed prisoners. I trust you realise your responsibilities and what we expect of you." He paused. "And what your friend here expects and hopes of you."

Jimmy looked aghast. He rubbed his head nervously and glanced at Jack.

Jack's face was chalk-white. Jack felt his stomach churn and he felt nauseous. He gagged and put his hand to his mouth.

"We were told we would be set free if we did this job for you," Jack said, trying very hard to control his trembling voice.

"That is correct," Panuf nodded.

"When do you want us to do this?"

"I'm not doing nothin' like that," Jimmy said firmly to Jack. He moved towards Panuf. "And you can't hang him over some sharp bits of wood if I can't do it. Look, boss," he pleaded, "I can't face heights. It's a serious medical condition, like. I can produce a medical note if you'll let me go back and get it."

Jack felt slightly embarrassed at Jimmy's display of cowardice. Nice try about going back for a medical certificate, he thought, but a bit of a bummer.

Panuf gave a sardonic smile. "Your bravery and loyalty to your friends is so much in keeping with the way you humans behave. I expected nothing different from one such as you. Full of bravado on the outside; like quivering jelly within."

He clapped his paws and two guards entered.

"Take this boy away," he ordered, pointing at Jimmy. "He does not seem to fully understand what is required of him. He needs to be convinced. Have Jago employ his techniques in persuasion."

72

The guards marched a protesting Jimmy out of the chamber.

Panuf turned to Jack and gave him an ingratiating smile. "I am sure you will understand that your co-operation will not go without reward. I repeat that in return for your help, we will release all of you so that you may return home to your families, who are no doubt extremely distraught at your disappearance. If for whatever reason that boy is unable to go, should Jago be too persuasive in his task, then you will have to convince the other one to do it alone. We would prefer two boys to undertake this task. This ensures greater likelihood of success. But I have every confidence that Jago will make your companion see reason. I leave it to you to convince your friend that co-operation is the only path open to you."

He clapped his paws again. Several other guards appeared. "Take this young human out onto the beach. Give him time to look around at the cliffs so he can see the lie of the land. Do not hurry him. Then return him to the holding cell." Panuf smiled at Jack. "My guards will push your chair to the beach. When you are looking around I suggest you do so without making it obvious to any watching Magars that you are assessing the cliff area. Anyway, it's getting dark so your presence on the beach should not be that obvious. Think carefully. Your decision will affect the continued life and freedom, or otherwise, of you and of your companions."

13

There must have been close to two hundred or so people who made up the slave labour force. Each group of fifty was allocated a prison cell and each group took it in turns, on a rota system, to be escorted to a large dining chamber, deep within the cave labyrinth, where other prisoners served them their meal. The doctor took Bill under his wing and now sat besides him at one of the long refectory tables occupied by another four persons. These other prisoners looked towards Bill and leant forward, as if to talk to him, perhaps ask more questions. Fournier shook his head, as if to indicate that they should leave the boy alone.

There were people of all ages, but no other children present. Neither were there any Rathings about. What little conversation there was was low and fitful. There wasn't even an occasional laugh. The diners ate their meal with eyes cast down and shoulders hunched. Bill found the sombre atmosphere disquieting.

The food was plentiful and tasty. Grilled mackerel with new potatoes and a green side salad and bread was followed by a choice of ice cream or sponge pudding and custard, all accompanied by cups of steaming-hot coffee or tea.

Doctor Fournier watched Bill tuck into his meal with relish. As the contents on the plate were quickly demolished, he smiled at the boy as he realised why the lad was so tubby. The doctor had never seen anybody clear a plate so quickly. "When did you last eat?" he asked kindly.

"Breakfast," Jimmy said, helping himself to another chunk of bread. "They do a good meal here, don't they? Do the Rathings always feed everyone so well?"

The doctor nodded. "At dinner, yes. It's in their best interests. They need to keep us well nourished so we can work hard. Breakfast and lunch are a bit meagre but dinner makes up for it. A few slaves are assigned permanently as cooks. They are the more fortunate ones. Slaving away in a kitchen is far more preferable to slaving away in the tunnels."

"What sort of work do we have to do?"

"They make us chip away at the rock face with pickaxes and hammers, enlarging their labyrinth of tunnels. Rathings breed so prolifically that they always need more living space. You may be fortunate that, being a child, sorry – a young boy – you'll be assigned to kitchen duties. If you're on tunnelling work you'll find it hard, backbreaking labour, but you'll just have to learn to grit your teeth and get on with it."

"Wouldn't it be a lot easier and quicker for everyone if they used pneumatic drills?" Bill remarked.

Fournier smiled at the logic of Bill's question. "Of course it would, but I suspect the general idea is to find gainful employment for people – or the masses, as they often refer to us humans. Unemployment and other State benefits were stopped when these creatures took over the country. Now everyone has to work, either in a paid job or press-ganged into slave labour, whether previously employed or not. With such a large pool of potential slave labourers the Rathings are not particularly concerned as to what kind of persons are captured or how long a job takes, as long as it is being done.

Bill nodded. This was something he had not been aware of, strange as it all seemed.

"Oh, incidentally, working alongside us will be a great number of Droons," Fournier continued. "I'd better warn you about them because they're another set of clones that you will never have seen as they never leave the confines of Rathings' quarters. They are an aberrant species of Rathing, a mistake made in the experimental work of the scientist who created them. You'll find them odd because their facial features are human as are their bodies, which are deformed and twisted at the waist. They have short, spindly ratlike legs and feet but no rat's tail. Droons are only about a metre tall and move with a shuffle or hop, skip and jump. Just a warning of what to expect."

"I've heard of Droons, but never seen any. They sound gross."

"Droons have always been held as slaves by the Rathings and forced to live in appalling conditions in subterranean parts of the cave network deep underground. I had to go down there once with a work party. It was shocking. Hordes of Droons were crowded together like a herd of pigs in an asphyxiating sty. Their living quarters – although 'living' is a misnomer – are dark, dank and disgusting."

"D'you know something, doctor?" Bill said. "I've never grasped why Rathings like to live in caves? I know they work in offices but why do they go home to caves? They rule the country. I mean, they could live in any house they like, even in Buckingham Palace now that we don't have a king."

"You're right about their working in office buildings. You can't govern a country or operate international communications, phones, computers, and email and so on from a cave. And besides which, they have to oversee and issue orders to the thousands of people who run the infrastructure of the country; civil servants, if you like. That, incidentally, is why the Rathings wear jerkins and skirts. They don't feel comfortable being naked in the presence of humans. But I understand they are quick to throw off their clothes once they get to their home. Anyway, they prefer their homes to be in caves because of the ratlike nature that is predominant in Rathings, much more so than the human part of them. They grow up in caves and that is what they are familiar with. They feel very much more at ease in caves, using the equivalent to rat-runs, if you like."

Bill took a sip of water and scratched his head. "How did these clones come about in the first place? I mean, how did it happen?"

"How did it happen?" Fournier raised his eyebrows and smiled. "Because of a madman." He leant forward, placed his elbows on the table and interlocked the fingers of his hands. He extended his thumbs under his chin and sat quietly, staring into space. Eventually, he spoke. "Many years ago, a group of scientists were working on stem cell research and reproductive cloning. Exerpiments – many of them secret – were being undertaken all over the world, especially in the early part of this century. At that time the odd snippet appeared in the press and on television and this news caused unease amongst the more enquiring minds of the population. There were loopholes in the law that allowed scientists to create clones by crossing humans and animals. No legal safeguards existed. People were justifiably worried because they were afraid of the unknown. What, they wondered, could be created if there were no controls in place?" Fournier gave a cynical laugh. "Little did they realise that one deranged scientist would, in fact, design that very abomination they had feared – monstrosities conceived through curiosity – our present government and lawmakers, our rulers."

"So cloning was wrong?" Bill asked.

Fournier shook his head. "No. Not in principle. There is nothing wrong with the concept of genetic engineering, and never has been. Man has always strived to attain new goals, make new discoveries, reach unknown horizons and genetic engineering is one of them. What posed a danger was how man handled his discoveries. If moral principles were ignored in favour of scientific application alone, then the relevance of the discovery, the manner in which it was used, was wrong, not the subject."

"D'you mean because of what some scientists were doing? Like the one who made these clones?" Bill stated, as he sipped his cup of tea.

"Exactly. Like our unprincipled scientist, a Professor Jens Andersen. He learned that in the late 1990s an American scientist, Dr Stuart Newman, submitted a patent application to meld human and animal embryos. These combinations included a man and a mouse, a human with a pig and with a baboon. Andersen also read that in 2003 China had successfully produced hybrid embryos by inserting human DNA into rabbit eggs."

Bill could only mutter "phew!" under his breath.

Fournier smiled. "Phew, indeed, Bill. The only difference between the many scores of secret experiments going on at the time and Andersen's work was that he had developed artificially modified DNA which ensured that his genetic melding would not be rejected."

"So what exactly is reproductive cloning, Dr Fournier?"

"It is a technology used to create a creature that has the same nuclear DNA as another. You see, scientists transfer genetic material from the nucleus of a donor adult cell to an egg whose nucleus, and therefore its genetic material, has been removed. You follow what I'm saying?"

Bill nodded. "Sort of."

"OK. So obviously the reconstructed cell containing the DNA from a donor cell must be treated. This is usually with chemicals or electricity to stimulate cell division. When the cloned embryo reaches a certain stage, it is transferred to the uterus of a female host where it continues to develop until birth. Fine so far?"

Bill shrugged. "I guess."

"Professor Andersen created the Rathings, Magars and Droons and he bypassed the process of transferring the cloned embryos to a uterus. His experiment was taken a stage further. He knew all about the complete genome sequence for both humans and rats. He had also established the location, sequence and function of each gene, each encoding a particular protein that produces a species' specific physical features. He then knocked out these specific human genes and replaced them with rodent or avian genes that he knew the function of."

Bill's glazed eyes prompted Fournier to simplify this last statement by further explanation: "Let me give you an example, Bill. Knowing the human genome, Andersen was able to knock out genes responsible for, say, jaw formation or formation of fingers during the development of the embryo and replace them with the equivalent rat genes. So his clone had a rat's jaw and the thin scaly claws of a rodent. Are you beginning to understand the overall picture of Andersen's work?"

"Wowzer!" Bill exclaimed. "That seems like quite a job."

The doctor nodded. "Andersen wrote a paper asserting that it was possible to genetically produce a part-human, part-animal creature. He sought the assistance of an expert on cytogenetics and together they began their clandestine work."

"Cyto what?" Bill frowned.

Fournier smiled. "Cytogenetics is the study of chromosomes, the visible carriers of DNA, which is the hereditary material."

"I see," said Bill, who hadn't understood a word of it.

"Cytogenetics is a fusion science, Bill. It's very straightforward if you think about it. It is the joining of cytology – the study of cells – with genetics – the study of inherited variation."

"Uhuh," Bill said, still unsure of what the doctor was talking about.

"Think, Bill," Fournier continued encouragingly. "The word 'cyte' is derived from the Greek word *kytos*, which means hollow, because that's what a cell is. Therefore cytology means the study of cells. Yes?"

Bill nodded.

"And genetics is something you must know something about."

"Sort of," Bill nodded again.

"Sort of?" Fournier laughed. "Come on, Bill. Genetics is the study of heredity, as the genetic code is the system of storage of genetic information in chromosomes. Have you not touched on that at school? Or are you too young for that?"

"Yes," Bill nodded. "I mean no, we haven't been taught anything like that at school."

"No, of course, you are a bit too young. Well, there you are. Andersen and his associate's experiments produced embryo clones with the head of a rat, enlarged to carry a human brain and borne partly by a human body. Only this body would have the specific features of a rat. A tail, for example, or rat fur and instead of human toes, long rat ones. He did the same to genetically engineer the Magars by interweaving the genes of a magpie and a human. Andersen and his associate called their experiment the Kytos Project."

"But didn't anyone notice what he was doing?" Bill frowned.

"No. He was clever. He worked late at night when alone in the lab. He washed away official, approved clones from plates and replaced them with his own. He placed them in the freezing compartment and openly introduced them into the growth tanks the following day. His experimental embryos grew and developed in the warm darkness. And he created three sets of mutant clones. One set – the Droons – did not quite turn out as the scientist had envisaged."

"I still don't understand why he did this. What was the point?" Bill looked perplexed.

"Put simply, the man was a bit deranged. As I said, in the past, many people expressed concern about cloning experiments. All it needed was one irrational scientist to play around with things he couldn't control, and there you have it. And now these mutant clones are our rulers."

"How come you're so clued up on what this scientist guy did?" Bill queried.

"Because I'm a scientist and I've read a great deal about it. Anyway," Fournier continued, "after early development in growth tanks, Andersen had to relocate the embryos elsewhere so that they would evolve naturally and he deposited them here, at Rumrunner Cove, with the agreement of the man who owned this place at the time."

"How did these clones become so advanced? You know, like speak English and use tools and weapons?" Bill asked.

"Andersen wanted to prove his theory that human and animal genes could be combined using modified DNA. Once this was successfully achieved, he had to locate the embryos somewhere and he wanted to see how they would evolve, just as early man did.

"Andersen realised that the clones had the potential to evolve more quickly than normal as they possessed the already advanced human gene. It wouldn't – and didn't – take them long to adapt to using tools, for example, or to establish a hierarchical society. But he also wanted to be sure that his clones could communicate and be understood by humans, so he successfully genetically programmed both the Rathings and the Magars to speak the human language, although the Rathings' style of speaking is a bit archaic and pedantic. You see, their brains were designed to be part human and part rat or magpie. That is why they may appear to behave as a human before their animal instinct takes over."

"You can say that again," Bill screwed his eyes up. "Having Rathings around is like living with giant, super-intelligent rats. You sometimes forget that they're partly human, like you and me."

"Very true," the doctor agreed. "Within a short time the Rathings became the dominant clones. They enslaved the Droons and treated the Magars as an inferior breed. Interestingly, Andersen bequeathed Shibboleth to only the Rathings. It was as if he knew this would happen."

Bill had been looking around curiously at the group of prisoners, many of whom had finished their meal and were returning to their prison cell.

"So what exactly is this Shibboleth they always talk about?" Bill turned his attention back to the doctor.

"Shibboleth is the formula of their creation. The Rathings have always considered Andersen as their god and refer to him as God Andersen. He gave them the formula with instructions to revere it as his instrument of their origination, their creation."

"He doesn't sound like a nice man, you know, creating these mutant clones," Bill began gnawing at his fingernails.

"He was a megalomaniac. He wanted to play at being God. He called it his Genesis – establishing his own universe and seeing how his creations would evolve and inter-relate with each other."

"The Rathings and Magars?"

"Yes. Given their genetic heritage, the two clones species are very different of course. Unlike the ordered structure of the Rathings, the Magars live in a loose-linked non-hierarchical society. They exist on a day-to-day basis and are so laid-back about most things that they're practically horizontal. The only things they're not relaxed about are their fights with the Rathings. It seems they really look forward to these skirmishes. But, from all accounts, these troubles seem to only exist here, not elsewhere in the country."

Bill was grateful to the doctor for his explanations. It made the existence of the mutant clones a little bit clearer. He reached out for another chunk of bread and began to pick at bits of the soft dough which he rolled into little balls between his fingers and popped into his mouth.

Fournier was quite impressed how Bill had seemingly come to terms with his imprisonment and the stark future ahead of him. The boy had a kind, honest, open face and possessed none of the cockiness usually evident in young people. He was a pleasant boy, Fournier thought, but extremely nervous and seemed to be unsure of himself. This was apparent by the constant biting of his fingernails.

Fournier thought he might get Bill to relax by engaging in some casual conversation. "Tell me, Bill. What d'you hope to do when you leave school?"

"Oh, that's easy. I've got it all planned. I want to go to university and study medicine."

Fournier smiled. "Excellent! A wonderful vocation. Is that what your father is – a doctor?"

Bill shook his head. "No. He runs a boat-building business. Has about twenty men working for him."

"I see," Fournier nodded. "You know, not many people realise how fit you have to be as a doctor. The hours are long and the work exacting."

Bill nodded. "I'm very strong, you know. Only my muscles don't show as they're hidden by all this." He pinched his tummy with both hands. "Not like Ashok. His muscles aren't hidden. He says he wants to be a cricketer, like his dad, but I know that he really wants to be a sound and acoustics engineer or something like that."

"Is that your friend?" Fournier asked.

"Yes, he's with the Magars."

Fournier looked surprised. "I thought only you had been captured. You mean the Rathings got two of you?"

"Four," Bill corrected. "There's Jack and Jimmy, although Jimmy isn't a friend. I don't know what Jack wants to do when he grows up. He's got spina bifida and has to use a wheelchair. Wouldn't be surprised if he doesn't become a concert pianist. He's very good playing the piano, you know."

"*Mon Dieu!*" Fournier exclaimed. "They've captured four children? Unbelievable!"

"Well, it was our fault really," Bill shrugged. "We came through the cave, which we shouldn't have. They found us on their beach." Bill started nibbling his fingers again.

Fournier shook his head. "That was a foolish thing to do. I thought the Rathings captured you in one of their raids. You poor children. This is most terrible."

Fournier looked at Bill and gave him a reassuring smile. "Tell me, Bill, why do you bite your nails?"

Bill shrugged. "Dunno. I've always done it. I guess you might say that the Rathings are pretty smart, sort of having taken over our country."

"Their sheer size and numbers, and the speed of their attack on the human population took us all by surprise. They had somehow acquired a range of weapons – it was never established how. They were quite inept at using them, but their main arsenal consisted of explosives, and they were more than efficient in that department. They bombed indiscriminately, killing thousands. They overran the country in a matter of weeks. I remember the fear and panic at the time. My wife and children managed to make it back to France. I was not so fortunate."

"That must have been awful. Terrible." Bill was really shocked.

"It was. There was complete carnage. Thousands of deaths, the military forces annihilated, government ministers executed. It was sheer good fortune that your king and family were able to make their escape to Canada." Fournier shook his head sadly at his recollection of those terrible events. "Yes, Bill, it was awful. And, sad to say, it's not good now." He gave a soft laugh, full of bitterness and regret. "The Rathings may claim that whilst they rule the country they do leave us free to lead our lives as before. True in some measure, but utter nonsense in the broadest sense. The human population is in reality little better off than serfs were in the Middle Ages. And as for us? What hope is there for prisoner slaves? We do not even have the comfort of knowing that our sentence is for a set period. We are here for life. There is no way out of this hell-hole until death decides to call on us."

He noticed Bill's frightened look. "I'm sorry, Bill. It is no use pretending to you that things will get better."

"You mean no one ever leaves here?"

Fournier nodded, and then gave a very Gallic shrug. "Ah, but the human spirit is amazing. Even though there seems to be no hope, the spirit keeps us going in the belief that one day things will change, will get better. We don't give up the will to live. That urge to cling to life is evident in each one of us here, young and old. We may sometimes want to curl up and die, but our spirit shouts 'No! No! Fight on!'"

Fournier suddenly seemed to regret his outburst. "I'm sorry, my young friend. Ignore the ramblings of an old man."

"That's OK," Bill said. "I understand how you feel. We're in a bad way, aren't we?"

"No. No. Not so bad that we can't have a game of chess before we bed down for the night. Oh, you do play chess, don't you?"

Bill nodded.

"Splendid!" Fournier clapped his hands in pleasure. He pulled out of his trouser pocket a small box containing primitively made wooden chess pieces and a chequered board. "A prisoner made this travelling chess set and left it with me. I always carry it around." He laughed. "It's my equivalent of a baby's comfort blanket."

"Did he die?" Bill asked. "I mean the prisoner who gave you that."

Fournier nodded. "Yes. He was executed," he said softly. "Still. One can always forget life's little problems when you play a game of chess." He got up. "Come on, young man. It's time we returned to our cell."

He smiled to himself as he saw Bill surreptitiously stuff into his pocket a couple of pieces of bread.

14

Ashok was dozing fitfully. His tummy rumbled from hunger, as the small amount of meat he'd been given some hours before hadn't really sated his appetite. He had a humdinger of a headache, his body ached all over, and the evening chill was beginning to finger its way through his thin T-shirt.

He laid his head back against the rock face and closed his eyes once again. His thoughts meandered, plucking out salient memory pictures of recent events: of their game of cricket on the beach, of their being captured by the Rathings, of the elderly man who lay badly wounded near by. Suddenly Ashok missed his family. He yearned for his dad and mum's comforting presence. They had been a real encouragement to him. He was determined to play County cricket like his dad had done before retiring and becoming the manager of the local building society, and they had been right behind him. Ashok was a fine sportsman, a valuable team member of his school's cricket 1st XI and rugby 1st XV. His sports master had told Ashok that he had a brilliant future ahead of him in either of the sports but Ashok dreamed of one day wearing his whites at Lords, just like his dad had done. He also thought of his girl-friend, Ellie. He recalled how she always turned up with a crowd of other girls to watch him play in cricket or rugby matches, and the pride he felt when she cheered louder than anyone else when he either hit a six or scored a try. He thought of their visits to the movies or their chats over tea at Mrs Lacey's Diner. He smiled, as he saw her worried face float before him. 'Don't worry, Ellie,' he said to himself. 'We'll all be back soon.' He then dozed off again, his mind a jumble of tumbling worries.

Ashok was suddenly aware of the presence of one of the Magars sitting next to him. He gave a startled jump.

"Sorry. Didn't mean to frighten you," the Magar apologised.

"Oh, I was just dozing," Ashok explained with a grin.

The Magar introduced himself. "My name's Rough Bird. How are you feeling?"

Ashok shrugged and shook his head. He looked at his watch. The time showed 11.55. He frowned and tapped the watch face. The second hand didn't move. He reckoned the watch must have broken during his escape to the cliff top. He looked up at Rough Bird. "Bit of a muddle," he replied. "I'm not sure I really know what is happening. It's all strange."

"I suppose we do look a bit strange to you," Rough Bird acknowledged. "Most of you humans wouldn't have come across us."

"No, no, I didn't mean that. I meant what's been happening. You've all been kind to me."

"I woke you to tell you that one of your friends is on the beach."

Ashok sat up straight. "Where? Can I see him?"

"Crawl towards the cliff edge and look down. He's in a chair with some Rathings."

Ashok moved to the edge and peered over. He could just make out the figure of Jack.

Ashok waved wildly. "Jack!" he called out. "Over here, man."

He saw Jack quickly wave back at him. Then the Rathings surrounded Jack and took him back into their cave.

"I'm really worried about my friends," Ashok said.

"I can understand," Rough Bird said. "The Rathings are cruel. But if your friends obey their rules, they won't be harmed. They'll make them work building tunnels but they'll feed them well as they want human prisoners to be fit for hard work. They certainly don't feed us when we are captured in battle, or the Droons, for that matter."

"Why do you and the Rathings fight?" Ashok asked. "There didn't seem to be any love lost between you when you came to rescue us."

Rough Bird shook his head. "I don't understand what you mean about love lost."

"Oh, it's just an expression. You seem to hate each other."

"We didn't once. It all began when our babies, who were too young to fly properly, fell out of the nest on to the beach and were caught and eaten by Rathings. We moved nests away from the cliff edge, but babies tend to roam about and sadly it still happens from time to time. We could never forgive such acts. We are now sworn enemies."

"Yep, I reckon I'd go along with that," Ashok agreed. "It's not nice seeing your kids being eaten by rats."

"And it became worse. Look down there, for example." Rough Bird pointed towards the poles with objects skewered on top.

"Yes, we were wondering what they were."

"On top of those poles are heads. Heads of executed Magars, as well as of Droons and humans."

Ashok gave a little shudder. "Heads? That's gross."

Rough Bird looked puzzled. What was this word "gross"? He continued: "Those who offend the Rathings, for whatever reason, have their eyes gouged out and their head cut off and placed on those poles."

"Gosh! That's really yuk!" Ashok exclaimed.

Rough Bird shook his head. The word "yuk" was also unknown to him. He thought that humans sometimes spoke a strange language.

"Go on," Ashok prompted.

"Humans are subjected to the same gruesome method of execution, except that humans and Droons are drowned at high tide after their eyes are taken out and before their heads are cut off." Rough Bird shook his head in sorrow.

"That is really, really mega, mega sick," Ashok whispered and shook his head. "But why do they drown the others but not Magars?"

"They know we would rescue any Magar tied to the drowning post."

"But not humans or Droons?"

"That is correct. The Rathings take particular pleasure in inflicting pain. And the Rathing overlord, Vadek, is the worst Rathing of all. He is very devious. I remember that Horos once asked to meet under a flag of truce." Rough Bird pointed with his wing towards a Magar who stood some distance away. "That's Horos, over there."

"Is he the boss-man around here? Er, sorry, I mean your leader?" Ashok asked.

Rough Bird shook his head. "It is not our way to

have any one Magar lead the rest of us. Each Magar conducts his life as he wishes, provided he does no harm to another Magar. But when one of us has an idea or a plan, we discuss it with others. Horos is always full of ideas and he usually talks with me about them."

"Sorry to have interrupted," Ashok grinned at Rough Bird. "You were saying about a flag of truce."

"Ah, yes. Well, Horos and I wanted to arrange a ceasefire between us and the Rathings. We told Vadek that Magar and Rathing should live in peace and that there was little point in continuing our skirmishes. We were prepared to forgive them for having caught and eaten our babies if they assured us it would not happen again. Vadek listened to what we had to say then told his guards to arrest us. He was quite happy to break all the rules of truce."

"That isn't on," Ashok frowned. "So what happened?"

"Fortunately, General Garbath was at the meeting. He told Vadek that it wasn't honourable behaviour to arrest us when he had agreed to meet under truce terms. Garbath called some of his soldiers and told them to escort us out of Vadek's chamber and return us to the beach." Rough Bird smiled. "I don't like any Rathing but I hold much respect for Garbath. He has that rare quality in a Rathing – honour."

"Well, he did the right thing," Ashok said.

"Unlike Vadek. Vadek is as cruel to his own kind when he decides to punish one of them. He occasionally sends a Rathing who does something wrong through a Time Gate."

"What's that?"

"Haven't you heard of the Time Gates?" Rough Bird seemed surprised.

Ashok shook his head.

"Time Gates transport any object either forward or back in time. No one Time Gate can do both. Some Time Gates send you back many years, whilst others shift you into the future. Because the Rathings know what the past was like, they only use those gates."

"I've never heard of them before."

"That's possibly because there are only about half a dozen, all in secret locations. Only some very senior Rathings know where they are located."

A sudden idea struck Ashok. "So, what you are saying is that if I, just for suppose purposes, decided I wanted to go back in time I could do so through a Time Gate?"

Rough Bird nodded. "If you know where to find one."

"Do you know?"

Rough Bird cocked his head to one side. "Is there a purpose to your question?"

Ashok thought it inappropriate to voice his thoughts. "Er, no. Just curious."

"Yes, I do know." Rough Bird didn't sound too convinced by Ashok's explanation.

"Are you the only Magar who knows, then?"

"Yes," Rough Bird said. He had an inkling what the boy was thinking. He certainly didn't like the idea of a young human attempting something dangerous like going into the past or the future through a Time Gate. Rough Bird looked somewhat annoyed.

Ashok thought he'd change the subject quickly. "Why do you leave the heads of your friends on those poles and not steal them and bring them back here?"

"What purpose would that serve? The head is life-less. But we do believe that a dead Magar lives on in this life."

93

Ashok gave a puzzled scowl. "How's that, if they're dead?"

"Their body may be no longer with us but the memory of them remains. We often speak of our dead companions. We mention their names in conversation. Sometimes we even talk to them aloud, asking their opinion. They remain very much alive to us. And whether dead or alive, we clones weep at the cruelty of you humans in having ever created us."

"I'm sorry? I'm not with you there," Ashok said.

Rough Bird shook his head. "Do you think that we – or the Rathings for that matter – can be really happy? The human who created us clones played a very cruel trick on us. We are neither one creature nor another. Our minds are often confused. Sometimes, like now, my young friend, as I speak with you I feel just like you, a human. At other times I am avian; I behave and react as a bird would. But in reality I cannot understand proper birds and they, in turn, find us alien, as you humans also regard us. We are oddities – neither one thing nor the other. And the same holds true for Rathings, who are neither rodent nor human. Rathings cannot communicate with their rodent cousins. Call a Rathing a rat and he considers it the greatest insult. Call him a human and he knows you lie. Is that not a heartless game that someone played?"

"I'm sorry," Ashok said quietly. "I never thought about it like that. I never realised the pain you must suffer."

Rough Bird shrugged. "But it is life," he said, "and we have learned to accept it. There is no other option. Apart from death perhaps, and that is why we never forget a Magar who has died."

Ashok nodded. "I suppose it's the same for us in some ways. I often hear adults talking about friends or family who have died. They say things like 'remember how so and so did this or said that'."

Rough Bird laughed. "There you are, perhaps we are not so different after all."

Ashok smiled at Rough Bird's feeble attempt to apologise for his outburst.

"I know that when I die I will still be here with my friends. It is a comforting thought. The man lying there . . ." Rough Bird indicated with his head. ". . . He was condemned to death. We made an exception in his case and rescued him from the drowning post. Horos had the idea that it might annoy the Rathings. The poor man is brave in having wanted to escape even though he cannot see."

"I was wondering about that," Ashok interrupted. "I thought something was wrong because of the bandage and the uncertain way he moved his hands in front of him. Then he told me he had his eyes put out."

"We feel sorry for him," the Magar continued. "He is in great pain from the spear injury but there is little we can do for him. We think he will probably be dead within the next day or so. His pain and troubles will then be over. But as you say that you humans also talk about those who have died, perhaps he will not be forgotten and his friends will continue to speak of him."

"That's a nice thought," Ashok agreed.

Ashok heard a commotion coming from the beach. He and Rough Bird crawled to the cliff edge and looked down. Several Rathings were jumping up and down in anger, shaking their paws towards the cliff. Rough Bird looked towards where the Rathings were directing their display of anger. He laughed. "Look over there!" He indicated with his wing to a spot where several Magars stood, holding a cylindrical gold tin in the air and shaking it about.

Ashok's gaze followed his pointing wing. "What's happening?" he asked.

"That tin held Shibboleth, the formula of their creation given to them by their creator."

"It belongs to them?"

"Yes. But we have it now. Well, the tin. We destroyed the formula." Rough Bird gave a loud cackle of laughter.

"How come you have it?"

"We stole it," Rough Bird said.

"You stole it? Why?"

"Oh, to make them angry. We wanted to annoy them and to gain revenge for all our companions who have been murdered by them. And to infuriate them further, we keep the tin in full view of the Rathings, even though it's empty. It frustrates them to see it there, thinking Shibboleth is still wrapped inside, and knowing that they can't get to it."

Rough Bird rose. "Get some rest now," he said gently. "In a few hours we will be flying down to the beach and will make a surprise attack on the Rathings. We will raid their stores for grain and seeds, which we need. We do this from time to time, but now is ideal because we saw a large number of their soldiers move away from their quarters and go towards the northern end of the beach. It puzzles us why they do this. Perhaps they are searching for the freedom fighters."

"It could be because of their ratlike nature," Ashok suggested, "You know, always moving around their territory, always sniffing and searching about."

Rough Bird shrugged. "That may be. This means there won't be as many guards as usual. If you want to watch, you'll have a grandstand view from here."

"Who are the freedom fighters?" Ashok asked.

Rough Bird gave a cackled laugh again. "They're a group of humans who sneak onto this beach from time to time. They keep blowing up the entrances of the Rathings' caves, or shooting at any Rathings on the beach with quick-firing weapons."

"Wicked!" Ashok exclaimed. "I'd never heard about them."

"There's a lot that takes place at Rumrunner Cove that you humans aren't aware of. Vadek doesn't run things here as he does elsewhere in his County. It's like another world at Rumrunner Cove."

"Tell me, why d'you need to steal food from the Rathings? Don't you have enough food then?"

"Our diet is mainly of beetles, worms, spiders and flies as well as other insects. But our numbers grow daily and there is not enough food around. We also enjoy eating small mammals but these are even rarer. I suppose we could fly somewhere else, to other cliffs, but this is our home and, anyway, other places would be already occupied by Magars. It is easier for us to take what we can find from the Rathings' stores. Besides, it annoys them, and that can't be bad."

"So what was that you gave me to eat?" Ashok asked with a worried look.

"Rabbit. Did you not like it?"

"Oh yes, it was good," Ashok replied but didn't add that it had been hardly cooked.

"Is there anything I can get you?" the Magar asked.

"No thanks. I just have one question. Is there any

chance that you could rescue my friends when you go down there?"

"Not easily. We try not to interfere where humans are concerned. Rathings are the rulers of the land. If they require slave labour, then so be it."

"I just can't sit here doing nothing," Ashok said angrily. "You must take me down to the beach with you. While you do your raid or whatever I'll try to set my friends free."

The Magar smiled and shook his head.

"No, I'm serious." Ashok placed a hand on one of the Magar's wings. "If you think you can't do anything to help them, then I am the only hope my pals have."

Rough Bird put one of his large wings on Ashok's shoulder. "Learn to be patient, my little friend. Life is not a direct line that is set down in stone. It is like a pattern drawn in the sand. Winds and shifting sands alter the design. And so do events in one's life. Be patient. Wait. Something will happen, I am sure." He stopped talking suddenly and cocked his head to one side, as if straining to listen to some sound. "And something else is happening down there," Rough Bird added, watching the beach intently. "Look."

The fracas that had taken place just a minute or so ago between the Magars waving Shibboleth at some Rathings had ended. The Rathings had returned to their cave. But Rough Bird noticed some movement on the beach. "Look down there," he whispered. "Against the rock face."

Ashok strained his eyes. He couldn't see much in the gloom. Then he made out some shadowy, creeping figures. It was a group of about a dozen people. They moved stealthily, carrying heavy canvas bags.

"The freedom fighters," Rough Bird whispered.

"Wow! Do you see them often, then?"

"Oh yes. We give them every encouragement and help, when needed. Anyone who fights the Rathings is a friend. We know their leader, Harry Carter. One of the best humans one would want to meet. A good friend. And he's a really funny man. He smiles and laughs all the time. He treats everything like a game, a big joke, despite the danger he and his friends face."

"But they don't live up here with you, do they?"

Rough Bird shook his head. "No. They live in small caves all over the coast and never stay in the same one for more than a few days. They are always on the move, and making lightning strikes to frustrate Vadek. But the freedom fighters' speciality is blowing up cave entrances."

Ashok smiled. "I bet. I can just imagine how those Rathings must feel trying to dig themselves out of the blocked caves."

"Oh no, the Rathings don't do it. They use the slave labour force."

Ashok didn't look so happy. "So it can't bug the Rathings that much after all."

At the mention of the word "bug" Rough Bird thought of food, then was sure that the boy didn't mean that. Another peculiar human word? Rough Bird wondered. "It is an inconvenience for the Rathings but it is more work for the slaves," he said.

"So how can you now do your raid if the entrance is blocked?"

"Oh, there are many entrances to the Rathings' . . ." Rough Bird began to reply, but his words were lost in the booming sound of an explosion somewhere below them.

Rough Bird quickly rose from his prone position

99

and jumped up and down, flapping his wings with joy. Ashok saw other Magars leaping about on the cliff top or flying up, making the chaw-chaw-chaw sounding calls used by excited magpies.

Ashok noticed one of the people running away from the blast, looking upwards towards the cliff and raising his right fist like a footballer might do after scoring a goal.

"Harry!" Rough Bird shouted and waved his wings about wildly. "Toodle-pip, Harry!"

"Hi, Rough Bird!" Ashok heard the man call back. He pointed his first two fingers as if firing a pistol. "Bang, bang, bang, eh?"

"Bang, bang, bang," Rough Bird gave a cackling laugh.

"See ya around," the man yelled as he disappeared with his companions round a sand dune.

"Why did you shout out toodle-pip?" Ashok was puzzled by the unusual call.

Rough Bird gave another cackle laugh. "Oh, Harry taught me that. It means goodbye."

Ashok smiled at the seeming high regard Rough Bird held for Carter.

15

They took Jimmy to the torture chamber.

All kinds of wicked-looking instruments lined the cave walls: pliers, hacksaws, hammers, whips, sharp, pointed metal skewers and many more. A fire blazed in a brazier standing against one of the walls.

They tied him to the floor with heavy chains. A hard-muscled very large black-furred Rathing, standing nearly three metres tall, approached, holding a pair of pliers in his massive paws. Jimmy could not help noticing that the Rathing's human feet with rat toes were badly scarred and very dirty.

"Well, putrid, smelly human," the Rathing said, turning towards Jimmy, his eyes red pinpricks of hatred staring from his rat face, "do you want your fingernails or your toenails pulled out first, *before* we boil you alive?"

Jimmy was so frightened he gagged and was nearly sick. He was desperate to delay the impending torture. In an effort to do so, he let out a strangulated cry, rolled his eyes upwards till the whites showed, and his head flopped to one side as if he had fainted. He held his breath and waited.

His trick had worked.

He heard the big Rathing swear. "Take him away," the Rathing ordered. "He can't enjoy the pain unless he is fully conscious. Let him lie awake tonight imagining what waits in store for him." The Rathing torturer gave a deep chuckle of pleasure at the thought of the various ways he could inflict pain on the boy.

The anticipated delights produced dribbles of greygreen saliva from his foul-smelling mouth.

16

Panuf had decided to confiscate Jack's wheelchair and Jack was being carried along a torch-lit tunnel. As they rounded a corner, Jack saw a strange figure in the distance. It was quite small and had a human body and human face with hardly any mouth, just a small slit. The creature was twisted at the waist, almost like a corkscrew. It had the legs of a rat but no tail. It was naked and appeared to be placing fresh straw in one of the cells located off the tunnel. As the Rathing carrying Jack approached, the creature threw itself down on the floor, placed both hands over its head and gave a series of guttural shrieks. It was clearly terrified about something. When the Rathing reached the prone figure, he placed his foot against it and pushed hard so that the trembling thing toppled sideways. It remained perfectly still in a foetal position. Shrieks were now replaced by soft sobs.

Jack felt a great sympathy for the poor creature. It might have been horribly deformed and ugly but it still had feelings. A look of extreme anger flashed in his eyes and he shouted to the Rathing, "There's no need for that. It's cruel, unnecessary."

The Rathing carrying him stopped and looked down at Jack. He seemed to be genuinely surprised at Jack's reaction. "Female Droon," the Rathing sneered. He gave a loud laugh and kicked violently at the recumbent body. "Filth," he shouted down at the trembling Droon.

Jack could not help but realise that brutality was the main characteristic of the Rathings' character.

The Rathing carried Jack into the small cell he and Jimmy had occupied previously. Jack noticed, through the gloom, the dim outline of Jimmy hunched in the far corner.

"Jimmy!" he exclaimed.

"Hi, Cripple," Jimmy gave a worried grin and looked relieved to see Jack.

Jack winced at the nickname Jimmy had adopted for him. He knew it was not meant unkindly. It was just typical of Jimmy's flippant and undisciplined attitude to life. Jack hated being disabled. Sometimes he wept silently when he watched his friends or other people running around or playing football and having fun in general, knowing that such freedom would never be his. He felt like a caged animal, unable to enjoy absolute freedom of movement, always dependent on others. But he rarely made his pain and frustration evident. He laughed and joked with others as if there was nothing wrong with him. It was only at night, lying in the still darkness of his bedroom, that he sometimes allowed the tears to flow down his cheeks and tried to control his sobs so that his parents would not hear him.

"They've brought some food for us," Jimmy said, pointing to two bowls piled high with what appeared to pass as a kind of stew.

"Are you OK?" Jack asked as he crawled across the floor.

"I've had better times."

"What did they do to you?" Jack now sat besides Jimmy.

"I told 'em to just transfer me to the penthouse suite, like, but the fools got me reservation mixed up, didn't they?" Jimmy said sarcastically. "Bloomin' idiots took me to a cell instead, threatened to pull out me blinkin' nails and then boil me! I funked it. I'm really scared, Cripple."

"That's not like you," Jack gave a guarded laugh. "Being frightened."

"That's right, Cripple. But you'd 'ave to be bloomin' bonkers not to be scared witless by this mob."

"Agreed. Well, if it helps, I'm scared also," Jack murmured. "I don't like the thought of dangling over some sharp pointed sticks in the ground." He glanced around the cell. "I wonder if there's any way out of here?"

Jimmy looked down at Jack. "You won't get far without your chariot. What 'appened to it?"

"They took it away from me. You could always carry me, of course," Jack suggested.

Jimmy shrugged. "S'pose so. You don't look all that heavy. That is if there is any way out of this dump." He nudged Jack. "Listen, about what he said, hanging you over those poles, like. I reckon he's kidding, just to make us scared and do this job for him."

"Well, he's succeeded OK. I've never felt so scared in my life," Jack muttered.

They said nothing for a while, and then Jack exclaimed, "Hey! Guess who I saw?"

Jimmy scowled and shook his head. "Cut it out, mate. I'm not in a mood for 'I spy'."

"No, no. Seriously, guess who I saw? Ashok."

"Your Indian friend?" Jimmy sounded surprised. "Where?"

"That Rathing priest creature told his guards to take me out onto the beach to look at the cliff. It was getting a bit dark but I saw Ashok waving madly at me from the top."

"Blimey, so he's OK then?"

"Seemed like it. I'll tell you something else I saw just now."

Jimmy sighed. "OK then, tell me."

Jack described the incident with the creature that the Rathing had called a Droon.

"Are you saying that there are even more weird creatures around here as well as these rats and bird thingies? I tell you, Cripple, I don't know what I've done to deserve this."

The two boys continued to sit in silence, each nursing his troubled thoughts.

Eventually Jimmy remarked, "I could do with a drink."

"I don't think they'll offer us a Coke or anything like that," Jack smiled.

"I'd settle for a sip of water," Jimmy replied, rubbing his throat as if to emphasise his thirst.

"Sorry I dragged you into this," Jack said.

"Bit late now. Wasn' your fault though. It was me who decided to follow you."

"Why did you follow us, Jimmy?"

"I was being nosey, I suppose."

After a while Jimmy said, "I don't like this idea they have. Getting us into the bird people's land and expecting us to walk away with their tin god." He shook his head and then reluctantly admitted, "Listen, if you must know, I'm scared of heights."

106

"You can do it," Jack tried to reassure Jimmy. "I'm sure you can. Besides, we've no option really. I don't much like the idea of being suspended over wooden spikes either."

"And I'm bloomin' scared of those bird-thingies."

"You can only do your best," Jack winked at Jimmy. Yet he was deeply concerned that when it came to the crunch Jimmy would probably bottle out. He couldn't really blame him. Jack reckoned that even if he, himself, was not restricted to his wheel-chair the prospect of what they were being asked to do was daunting. He wondered if Panuf meant what he said he'd do to him if Jimmy and Bill failed. He silently cursed himself again for having agreed to them going through the cave.

Jimmy watched Jack from the corner of his eye. He had come to reluctantly admit that Jack wasn't the wimpy kid in a wheelchair that he'd see occasionally in the village. It's funny, Jimmy thought. Until you actually get to talk and share experiences with someone, you don't know what they're really like. He was surprised at how Jack was facing their prob-lems calmly, even bravely.

Jimmy was appalled at the described method of execution Jack faced if he and Bill failed in their task to retrieve Shibboleth. He knew that when it came to the crunch, he would have no option but to do what the Rathings wanted. But, in the meantime, he would do all he could to protest and avoid undertak-ing the mission. He felt sorry for Jack, whose life, or death, lay on the success or otherwise of a mission over which he, Jack, had no control. For a short while Jimmy's fear for himself was replaced by a fear for Jack.

But any kind of sentimentality always had a short

lifespan where Jimmy was concerned. He nudged Jack. "'Ere, listen, Cripple. What I've told you about me being scared of heights, like. That's just between the two of us, OK?"

Jack nodded.

"I don't know why I told you but if I ever hear your pals say anything, I'll know where it came from," Jimmy threatened.

"I won't tell anyone, I promise, Jimmy," Jack assured his companion. "Just call me Mr Zip Lips," he said as he drew his index finger across his mouth.

17

The egalitarian nature of the Magars' society waived the need for appointed leaders or chieftains. Each member of the community enjoyed complete freedom of choice to do as and how they wished in their daily activities. They did, however, recognise that some form of leadership was essential in their regular skirmishes or battles with the Rathings. They knew it was important to have a battle plan and imperative that they followed instructions from a designated individual who acted as a military commander. Horos and Rough Bird – possibly because of their strong personalities and forthright views – were invariably accorded the distinction of formulating tactics and leading any such engagements.

Horos was an extremely handsome creature, taller than most of the others and with a commanding presence. It was his nature to encourage action rather than order it. He and Rough Bird made a formidable team, and despite the professed equality of all members of the colony, most Magars looked to either Horos or Rough Bird for help, advice or guidance.

The Magars' attack was launched at precisely three in the morning. The beach was deserted and they had no difficulty entering the labyrinth of tunnels that led to the Rathings' living and sleeping chambers.

On this occasion the attacking force was made up of three groups. Rough Bird led the first, largest, detachment. Two other Magars, called Condor and Argon, each commanded the other two teams. In overall control was Horos.

Horos was puzzled. It had all seemed very easy. Where were the Rathings guards or lookouts? Why had no alarm been raised?

He beckoned Rough Bird over to him. "Something's very odd, Rough Bird," he whispered. "We've attacked them often enough and they have always had guards posted. Where are they tonight?"

Rough Bird looked up at Horos. "D'you think this is a trap?"

"Possibly. We must be more cautious than usual. Tell the troops to be very silent."

Horos was watching Rough Bird make his way back along the tunnel to speak with Condor and Argon when several doors burst open and a large number of Rathings rushed out, squeaking at the top of their voices. They held long pointed spears and a few rifles. Horos ran back to where the Magars had congregated. "They're attacking!" he shouted a warning. It looked like the Magars were trapped. The Rathings had deliberately allowed them to enter the tunnels where they held a definite advantage.

"We must get into the chambers or onto open ground," Horos shouted. "Retreat! Retreat!"

The Magars fell back in an orderly manner until they came out onto the beach.

As the Rathings rushed out at them, the Magars flew up and began their attack on the Rathings. This time, the Magars were better prepared. They had brought with them large boulders that they had left on the beach. They now collected a boulder under one wing and used the other, powerful wing to guide their flight. Even the protective shields held over their heads did not save the Rathings from being smashed to the ground by the hail of boulders.

The Magars had the advantage of conducting an aerial attack. However, advantage or not, several Magars were speared when they flew too low to peck at the faces and bodies of the Rathings. Horos was amongst the victims, having been speared in his right thigh. He fell to the sand and was about to be engulfed by several Rathings when Rough Bird, aided by two other Magars, swooped down and managed to fight off the Rathings approaching Horos.

Rough Bird then led a number of Magars into the tunnels. He and his companions fought their way into the various chambers. They raided the Rathings' Temple and Council Meeting chamber, breaking everything they could find. Large bags were slung around their necks and they filled these with grain and seeds, which they stole from the Rathings' food store. They smashed their way into the nurseries and, although they were unhappy to do so, they nevertheless killed as many Rathing infants as they could find. To permit the babies to live would only allow them to grow to adulthood and present an ongoing threat to the Magar colony. But the Droon nursemaids were spared. The Magars passed the cells occupied by the human slaves but they made no attempt to free them. The objective of the raid was to steal from the stores and kill infant Rathings. Their task did not include releasing human slaves. They did, however, find the cells that held a few Magar prisoners whom they released.

Horos was finding it very difficult to fly and attack the Rathings. He fluttered onto a low cliff edge and directed the battle from there. Argon joined him and offered assistance. Horos noted that his troops were gradually pushing the Rathings back into the tunnels and saw Rough Bird and some others come rushing out just in time. Rough Bird signalled that he had managed to inflict damage by drawing his wing across his throat.

Horos signalled his companions to end the battle, and as he turned around he saw his brother, Therros, stabbed through the chest by a spear held by a very large albino Rathing. "No!" he screamed, and made a feeble attempt to flutter down onto the beach. The Rathing who had stabbed Therros turned round and Horos immediately recognised Vadek. Vadek laughed and raised his bloodstained spear skywards. "You are next, Horos," he called out, and then turned to join the other Rathings running towards the tunnels.

The short skirmish was over. The Magars did not pursue the Rathings and they began making preparations to return to their cliff-top home.

Horos had by now managed to scramble back onto the beach and was cradling his dying brother in his arms when Argon came up behind him.

"I'm sorry, Horos." Argon placed a wing on his commander's shoulder.

"I want to take Therros back," Horos whispered.

"You're injured," Argon said gently. "Let me carry him home."

Horos looked up at his friend. "You are right. I can't manage this with my injured leg. Thank you."

Argon gathered Therros gently and, with Horos, joined the rest of the Magars on their flight home.

18

Rathing guards entered the cell very early in the morning and dished out bread and lukewarm coffee. The prisoners wolfed down their meagre rations and were then gathered into a number of work parties.

Bill had had a very restless night. The dire situation in which he found himself preyed on his mind and he had tossed and turned on the thin layer of straw spread over the hard rock floor. The constant coughs, snuffles and movement of many other bodies intruded on his troubled drowsiness. His disturbed, shallow sleep had left him feeling lethargic, his movements slow and sluggish.

Doctor Fournier beckoned Bill to join him. "You'd better work with me," he said, "so I can show you what to do."

Bill joined the others who shuffled down a main tunnel. They were handed pickaxes and claw hammers at the entrance of a side tunnel. The tunnels were brightly lit with wall-fixed firebrand torches.

Bill saw wooden scaffolding already in place further down the tunnel. It was high scaffolding as the tunnel height had to be quite considerable so as to accommodate the gigantic stature of the Rathings. The prisoners began to climb the scaffolding.

Bill stood next to Fournier on the scaffold. They all

began chipping away at the rock face. It was slow, tiring work and the tunnel was soon filled with dust particles clogging their noses and making their eyes smart.

Bill saw a large party of Droons for the first time. They were completely naked and were working on another scaffold further down the tunnel. He was taken aback at the bizarre appearance of these creatures; the doctor had certainly not exaggerated their oddity. There were both males and females in the work party. Bill turned to Fournier. "Are those the Droons you mentioned?" he asked.

A startled look crossed the man's face and he scowled at Bill. He put a finger to his lips indicating silence and then looked around anxiously to see if any Rathings were within earshot. "No talking," he whispered urgently from the corner of his mouth, and continued hammering away at the rock face. Not once did he look directly at Bill.

They all worked on, chipping and hammering, hammering and chipping, on and on and on for what seemed like hours. The dust was now very dense and several of the people began coughing.

"Cease!" a Rathing guard ordered. "Water break."

Several Droons, who had not been in the Droon work party, appeared carrying buckets of water. They placed them at the foot of each scaffold. Slowly, the prisoners – humans and Droons – descended and began drinking from the buckets. There were no cups or any other type of receptacle so they cupped their palms and scooped water into their mouth. Rathing guards walked around. No one spoke.

After five minutes a Rathing shouted out "Commence!" and the workers began to climb the scaffolding and continue their labours.

At about noon the Rathing Work Master called a lunch break. All the prisoners scrambled down to the tunnel floor and waited for food to be brought to them by some Droons and humans who had not been working at the rock face.

It was a basic, watery kind of stew with indescribable blobs floating about which Bill was told later were dehydrated chicken cubes.

Bill was about to say something when he remembered the rule of no talking. He bit his tongue just in time, when he realised a Rathing guard had moved to stand directly behind him.

Work continued, with occasional water breaks. The heat was intolerable and the dust enveloped everyone, invading noses and eyes. The atmosphere was heavy and suffocating. At one stage, Bill heard a commotion coming from one of the scaffolds. He turned and saw a Droon leaning forwards precariously towards the rock face. His companions were trying to pull him back but he appeared to be intent on chipping at a particularly difficult protuberance. He kept shrugging them away. Bill thought the Droon was silly to lean well beyond the safety barrier. The Droon leant further forward and swung his pickaxe at the rock. And he lost his balance. With a terrible shriek, the Droon plummeted to the hard floor. The dull thud of body hitting rock shocked all the workers. The Droons began to wail and sway backwards and forwards in anguish.

A huge Rathing guard quickly mounted the scaffold in a couple of strides. He carried a horsewhip with which he flayed the cowering Droons. "Work. Go on. Work. No stop," he shouted.

Someone blew a whistle. Several Droons came running into the cave, whipped on by Rathing guards

115

who followed. The Droons were ordered to take away the broken, bloodied body.

Eventually some semblance of normality returned.

The sound of chipping and hammering continued until early evening when the order to stop was shouted by a Rathing Work Master.

The prisoners assembled at the foot of each scaffold and were marched out to the beach.

Humans and Droons alike stumbled towards the water and threw themselves into the sea. They splashed about, some diving under the waves, washing away the dust and grime that coated their bodies. None swam more than a few metres from the shoreline. A phalanx of Rathing guards stood in the water some distance out forming a tall and wide impassable barrier.

The Droons hopped, skipped and jumped back to their underground quarters and the humans were escorted back to their prison cells to await the call for dinner.

Back in the cell, Bill lay in an exhausted heap on some straw. He felt pain in muscles he never knew existed. His body screamed with fatigue. He was concerned that his dad would be frantic with worry at his disappearance. He also missed the comfort of having the other boys around him. The French doctor had been very kind to him, and he was grateful for the solace he'd received, but that could not totally calm his fear at having to face this situation on his own. Bill also worried how the others were coping. He was surprised not to see at least Jimmy working in the tunnel. What had happened to him and Jack since they were taken to see Vadek? Why had they not been returned to the small cell or even the large

116

cage that housed prisoners? Where were they? What had happened to them?

He recalled looking down from a great height at the broken body of the fallen Droon and seeing the widening carpet of red, as the blood flowed from the mangled figure that now resembled a broken string puppet. It was a shocking accident to witness. He could still hear the piercing scream of the Droon as he fell to the hard ground below. The callous attitude of the Rathings should not have surprised Bill, but it still did. His disjointed thoughts started to run out of control; he began to imagine the worst. He cradled his face between the palms of his hands to stop the warning pinpricks of tears that began to call for attention. I mustn't cry, he thought. Boys don't cry, even though they may be lost and desolate and in fear of their life and that of their friends. Bill did not like his tendency to shed tears when he found cir-cumstances stacked against him. He didn't know why he did this. He hated being thought of as a crybaby. He certainly wasn't that. He could be as tough as the next fellow. It was just this emptiness he sometimes felt when faced with situations he believed to be unfair and which he couldn't control. It was his uncertainty, his lack of self-confidence, his belief that he was not as good as others in dealing with problems. He doubted if he could cope with this regime of work, day in and day out for who knows how many months or years.

He wished he wasn't stuck in this awful place. He longed to be at home, his safe, cosy, comfortable home, with all the familiar sights and sounds around him.

He tried to breathe in slowly and deeply. He had to

think of something else; sitting here feeling quite desperate achieved nothing. His brooding gradually eased and he felt his body slowly relax. The muscle pain in his back started to nag and his stomach felt empty and in need of sustenance. His thoughts inevitably turned to food. He wondered what was for dinner; he'd really enjoyed the meal the previous evening. Images of large plates piled high with meat pie and chips began to dance invitingly behind his closed eyes. The image lingered tantalisingly then faded as he blissfully recalled the smell and taste of hot freshly baked bread. He remembered the times he'd walked home after visiting Brown's the Bakers, carrying a warm loaf and being unable to resist the temptation of picking chunks from the warm crust. First one corner would be attacked, then another. There was something awfully satisfying in sneaking bits of warm bread whilst strolling home. Usually, by the time he'd reached his garden gate, the loaf looked somewhat bedraggled and much smaller than it had been originally. Ah, he smiled. What would he do now for a lovely chunky slice of freshly baked bread?

Then this image vanished, not fading away slowly as that of the pie and chips had done, but sharply as he felt another twinge of pain in his back.

19

Vadek was furious.

"Where were you and several brigades of soldiers when the Magars attacked?" he demanded.

General Garbath adopted his usual delaying tactic; he did so now, placing himself in such a position that Vadek was berating him on his blind and deaf side. Of course, Garbath did not reply (although he had, in fact, heard Vadek very well, as Vadek was shouting and spluttering so loudly).

Vadek moved round to face Garbath. "I want to know where you and three brigades of soldiers were when both the rebels and the Magars attacked?"

Garbath shrugged his big shoulders. "We were on patrol at the north end of the beach and then searched the caves on Smugglers' Retreat," he replied.

"At that time of the morning?" Vadek snarled.

"Time means nothing to me and my troops. We may be anywhere at any time. As it was, we were trying to locate the whereabouts of the rebel band." Garbath smiled. "And it is regrettable that the Magars decided to attack at more or less the same time. In any case, brother," he added, "you know from experience that they can strike at any time. Weren't you ready for them, then?"

"Oh, yes, we were ready for them, General Garbath." Vadek addressed his brother by his title, as if to deliberately rebuff Garbath's earlier familiar form of address. "But you had taken half my soldiers with you. We were nearly defeated."

"*Your* soldiers?" Garbath raised an eyebrow. "I thought I was in charge of the army. Surely you mean *my* soldiers, don't you?"

"I am appointed Overlord. Every single Rathing, whether civilian or soldier, is answerable to me. Even you, Garbath."

General Garbath scratched his head and then shrugged his shoulders again. "I'm sorry I wasn't there with *your* soldiers to give you a total victory. Still, you seem to have managed quite well without me."

"Our Temple and stores destroyed!" Vadek shouted. "Nursery babies killed! Untold damage that will take ages to make new."

"Oh. Then you didn't manage quite so well, after all," Garbath replied.

"You are becoming extremely insolent, Garbath." Vadek walked over to his general. "I know very well what is in your mind."

"Really?"

"You deliberately removed a large number of our troops on a supposed fool's errand so as to leave us short-handed. You wish to undermine my authority so that you can assume the leadership. I am aware that you have been planning this for some time."

"I have been planning nothing," Garbath snapped. "The only one who undermines your authority is yourself. You and that toadying, sycophantic priest."

Vadek chose to ignore what Garbath had said. He continued, now in a menacing tone. "Don't try and deny it, General. My spies have kept me well informed as to what is going on. Because you are my brother I have continued to make allowances for your arrogance and insolence, which I would not tolerate from anyone else. But this time you have overstepped the mark. You have gone too far. This is no longer a matter of our disagreeing on the way things should be done. Your underhand action could have been disastrous to our colony. What you did can no longer be regarded as a personal attack on me, but an offence to all Rathings. This is nothing short of treachery."

"No, Vadek!" Garbath shouted. He placed his right paw on a dagger strapped to his waist but he did not unsheathe it. "This is not true. I took the troops out on a routine patrol. What you say is wrong, very wrong. I have never plotted against you, and I strongly object to your accusations of treachery. Why are you doing this, brother?"

The two Rathings were alone in Vadek's chamber. But the Rathings congregated outside could hear their raised voices and were aware of the gravity of the situation. A feeling of unease rippled through the listeners.

Vadek and Garbath faced each other. The atmosphere was taut with anger and hostility. Vadek had now also placed his paw on his sheathed dagger. He was very much aware that he and Garbath did not always see eye to eye but, deep down, Vadek had always found it difficult to fully accept that his brother was plotting against him. True, a handful of Rathings had suggested this, but Vadek sometimes wondered if they had their own agenda for creating this dissension between the two most powerful members of the tribe. There had been a definite unease within the tribe since Shibboleth had been stolen, and Vadek had been driven by fear ever since. Fear of his authority being weakened, fear of losing control, fear of failure, fear of losing respect. Vadek was becoming panic-stricken. Could he be losing his grip? Was his all-powerful status under threat? Was it possible that those senior Rathings, who had their own reasons to drive a wedge between the two brothers, had fed off Vadek's fears and had contorted facts to best suit themselves?

Fear has a habit of making one act unreasonably so as to protect oneself. And Vadek's fears drove him to make unreasonable assumptions. It was easier for Vadek to find a scapegoat in Garbath than to face his own uncertainties. Furthermore, this self-questioning was exacerbated by the long history of disagreement between the brothers. Vadek was determined to bring to an end the continuing, the endlessly prolonged dissension that existed between himself and Garbath. He decided that he had to act immediately if he was to strengthen his position as Overlord especially as others had been witnesses to Darma's words of reprimand. He felt that he had prevaricated for too long over his uncertainties concerning Garbath's supposed treacherous intentions. He had to demonstrate strong leadership qualities by taking decisive action. There was no time for further delay.

Fear can also make one act on the spur of the moment. And that is precisely what Vadek did. He strode to the door and flung it open. He beckoned to one of the senior officers who commanded his personal guard.

"You will arrest General Garbath on charges of treason and neglect of duty," he ordered.

20

A group of Rathing guards took Jack and Jimmy to
Vadek's chamber. Jimmy carried Jack, as Jack's
wheelchair had still not been returned to him.

Jack was surprised and delighted to see Bill
already there. The two friends exchanged hugs and
greetings. Jack told Bill about having seen Ashok
waving to him the previous evening. Jimmy stood
slightly apart, on the sidelines, feeling very much an
outsider.

Vadek entered, surrounded by a group of his
guards.

"How nice to see you all so happy. It brings such
joy to my heart." He waved his arms theatrically in
the air. "Co-operate with me, as you now do, and
you will find that I am not the monster you may
believe me to be." Vadek smiled broadly. "I can be
kind and understanding. That is why I am delighted
to grant you freedom to return to your homes. But
first I wish you to undertake the small task about
which some of you have already been told."

"And what's that?" Bill asked.

Vadek did not reply immediately. He walked to his
large chair and sat down. He leant his head back and
stared up at the high ceiling of the cave, gathering
his thoughts.

123

"He wants us to fetch his bloomin' tin from the cliff top," Jimmy announced.

Vadek looked down at Jimmy. He scowled and waved a crooked finger at the boy, beckoning him forwards. "Approach me, boy," he said quietly, but with more than a hint of menace in his voice.

Jimmy shambled forwards.

"Do you wish to make another visit to Jago?"

Jimmy shook his head repeatedly, terror etched all over his face.

"Then do not presume to speak for me."

Jimmy nodded.

"I wish for you to return Shibboleth to us," Vadek stated, addressing Bill.

"How?" Bill asked, his face screwed up nervously.

"We wish to create a believable situation which will not cause any suspicion to arise amongst the Magars. You will be allowed to be taken by the Magars to their cliff top. You will be told on what day we wish this to happen."

"You mean you'll let us join Ashok?" Bill said, trying not to betray the hint of excitement in his voice.

Vadek shook his head and frowned. "Who is this Ashok?"

"Our friend who was taken by the Magars when we first arrived and you captured us," Bill replied.

"Ah, yes, your friend with the Magars."

Bill scratched his head and turned to Jack. "Who has he in mind to do this?" he asked.

"You and Jimmy," Jack whispered back. He decided he would not tell Bill of the threatened punishment the Rathings had in mind for him.

Bill looked down and shrugged. "Yeah, I figured that. You couldn't do it."

"And I can't handle heights," Jimmy cut in, "so that leaves just you, Fat Boy."

"That's uncalled for," Jack snapped at Jimmy. "Why d'you always think it's smart to be rude?"

Jimmy gave an uneasy cough and turned to Vadek. "I really mean it, boss. I'd faint if I was to be up there. It's a medical condition called agrophob or vertigo or something, I think."

"Then we'll ask Jago to cure you of it, whatever this illness is that you have," Vadek said to Jimmy. He shook his head in mock astonishment. "I am sometimes amazed at the way you humans bicker amongst yourselves. You two . . ." He pointed at Bill and Jimmy. ". . . will be infiltrated into the Magars' encampment. Once you are there, we will give you a maximum of three days to familiarise yourselves with the area and to undertake the task required of you. Then we will create a diversion on the beach. That will be your signal. When the Magars are pre-occupied you will collect the gold-coloured tin and make your way down a side path with it or, if necessary, throw it down to us on the beach. You can see this path easily. It is too narrow for us but adequate for your size. I will ensure that there are sufficient soldiers to protect you in case the Magars decide to try and stop you."

"And what if we can't get hold of this tin? Or if the Magars learn of the plan?" Bill asked.

Vadek shook his head. "The Magars would only learn of this plan if you tell them. And that would be very foolish of you. You should have no difficulty getting hold of Shibboleth." He smiled and added, "Your incentive is to realise that your friend here" – he pointed at Jack – "will be quite safe as long as you do what we demand. If you disobey or fail . . ." He shrugged his shoulders and gave a chuckle. "Well, his life could no longer be guaranteed. If you accomplish your mission successfully, then we shall release you from your slave-labour duties."

"When are we going to have to do this?" Bill asked.

"Not for some days," Vadek replied. He didn't want them undertaking any such attempt until General Garbath had been dealt with. He wanted Garbath tied to the drowning post and finished off with beforehand. Vadek had already decided on his brother's fate even before a Court hearing.

"You really are some bozo. Looks like you hold all the cards in your hand," Jimmy spat out.

"And you hold the lives of your friends in *your* hand," Vadek smiled back.

21

The Rathings' Court had convened. Garbath, escorted by two guards, was obliged to shuffle into the Court chamber as his legs and paws were manacled. The indignity of his situation was not lost on the Court members. Garbath was told to remain standing between his guards whilst the charges against him were read out. He noted that all those seated before him were members of the tribe who held some animosity towards him. Vadek and Panuf had carefully orchestrated the hearing to suit their purposes.

Panuf put forward some very convincing arguments as to Garbath's guilt. He had also recruited false witnesses who were instructed to say that Garbath had told them on many occasions that Vadek was not making the right decisions and that he should take over as Overlord. Panuf even managed to convince the Court that Garbath had deliberately taken several brigades of soldiers to the north beach at the time of the attack by the Magars so as to leave the colony short-handed and make Vadek look incompetent. Panuf went on to suggest that, even if Garbath had not done so intentionally, Garbath was responsible for making sure that his sentries would not report on any intended attack by the Magars. Panuf accused Garbath of failing in his duty.

Vadek, wearing his policeman's hat tied around his chin with a blue ribbon, addressed the Court. He pointed out that Garbath had not managed to rescue Shibboleth from the Magars. Why? he asked. Because it suited Garbath's purpose for their godly symbol to remain with the Magars so as to put the blame on Vadek. Vadek said he believed that Garbath had instructed the soldiers not to succeed in their attempts. Vadek stressed that what was important was the safe return of Shibboleth. And Garbath had failed to do this. "Furthermore," Vadek continued, "at a recent meeting of the Council General Garbath virtually stated that he is no longer prepared to consider taking any steps to rescue Shibboleth. And there are witnesses to that clearly intended dereliction of his duties; namely, Captain Sarum, Superintendent Dalus and Commissioner Batanguma, not to mention our High Priest and Keeper of the Scrolls, Panuf, and, of course, myself."

Together, Vadek and Panuf had turned rumour and innuendo into apparent facts and had presented a convincing case against Garbath.

General Garbath was not allowed to say anything in his defence. When he began to protest and point out that the facts were not as presented to the Court, he was told to be silent. The Court found Garbath guilty and sentenced him to death. Owing to his status in the tribe, he was spared the indignity and pain of having his eyes gouged out before drowning. General Garbath looked at Vadek and the other members of the Court with contempt as he was led to the cells to await his execution.

22

All three boys were locked in a small cell. Vadek did not want them to mix with any of the other human prisoners in case they mentioned his plan, inadvertently or otherwise. He had also instructed that they were not to work on any tunnel building in the presence of other prisoners until the day of their supposed escape. Instead, they were assigned to work alone in a small cave area far removed from the main tunnelling activities until the day of the supposed escape, when they would be permitted to work in the main tunnel and bathe in the sea.

And so they existed for days on end, chipping away at the rock face. Even Jack, still without his wheelchair and carried everywhere by Jimmy, was obliged to sit on the cave floor and chip away at the lower level of rock face.

They were not allowed to bathe in the sea after their strenuous labours but were given buckets of water with which to wash themselves. They had only some rough brown wrapping paper and one bucket for toilet purposes. Rathing guards brought their meals to them.

Jack continuously thought of how they could escape from Rumrunner. There had to be an answer somewhere. Bill and Jimmy complained constantly.

Tempers flared, rows erupted and, on one occasion, blows were exchanged between Bill and Jimmy. It was when Jack gave vent to his frustrations, and snarled some very rude comments at Bill, that he was mortified to realise that they were all becoming quite savage in their behaviour. When he eventually tried to reason with the others, attempted to point out that they would lose their resolve to overcome their difficulties if they did not stand firm together, he was shouted down. Jimmy took the opportunity to remind Jack what he had once said. "Call me Mr Zip Lips, you said," Jimmy snarled, "so act the part and button it, mate, or I'll stitch them up for you."

23

General Garbath strained at the ropes that bound him to the pylon on the deserted beach. His chest muscles heaved, and the effort of trying to free himself was making him weak and tired. He was very tightly bound. The bright summer sun sparkled on the sea, the water reflecting the sun's brilliance like a mirror. The shimmering sand was beginning to burn his feet. After a long time of struggling he closed his eyes and his head slumped on his chest through sheer exhaustion. He resigned himself to his fate.

He was in this position when he heard the soft crunch of sand and approaching feet. He looked up and could just make out several figures advancing, crouched low and carrying weapons. He wondered if Vadek had decided to have him killed quickly, instead of waiting for the high tide.

"General," he heard a loud whisper. "It's Kera. We've come to rescue you."

His good eye squinted in the bright sunlight and he at last managed to make out the advancing figures as some of his soldiers, led by Kera, one of the most fearless warriors under his command. She held the record for having killed or injured the greatest number of Magars.

Kera was not a very tall Rathing and, despite her fearsome reputation on the battlefield, she looked demure and somewhat fragile. Her rat fur was a coffee-brown colour, her figure slim and elegant. She was a very pretty, young Rathing, and she often used her good looks to her advantage. When she spoke, she did so with a very slight lisp which Rathings found attractive. Her superiors also recognised that her strong personality and leadership capabilities qualified her as a suitable military commander. Her troops held her in high esteem and would do anything she asked of them.

Her best friend and constant companion, Xander, a swarthy, powerfully-built Commander in charge of the 1st Army Corps, followed behind her.

"General," Xander said, "the rest of the troops are hiding behind the sand dunes."

When Garbath was untied he tried to stand but fell on the sand through exhaustion. His officers picked him up and carried him to the sand dunes. Garbath was surprised to see that nearly all of the brigades, together with their Commanders, had gathered there, all of them in battle uniform and armed. The uniform of the Rathing soldiers varied. Some wore thongs of dried seaweed whilst others had bits of old rope strung about their shoulders. Officers wore over their shoulders small corks that, threaded together, looked like chain mail. Sometimes, especially in major battles with the Magars, Rathing officers painted their thongs and corks in bright colours. No insignias were worn; everyone knew who held what rank in their army. Their principal weapons comprised spears, swords, knives and daggers, but they also used stones and planks of driftwood as coshes or any other item they could lay their paws on which might be useful as a weapon for hitting. None of them carried rifles. They regarded such weapons as cowardly armaments, used by the inferior breed of humans. When a Rathing fought another, he did so face to face and close to his opponent. Guns were only considered suitable to kill Magars.

"We must leave here," Xander said. "We have set up headquarters in some of the caves at Smugglers' Retreat. The rest of your troops await you there. We've also appropriated large supplies of food from the stores, so we have sufficient rations to last a while."

General Garbath smiled and put his paw on Xander's shoulder. "You are a good friend," he said. "All of you are loyal friends," he continued, addressing the other rescuers.

"And we are here to help you destroy Vadek and bring back some order into our lives," Kera said. "How could he treat you like this? After all you have done! And you, his brother! We will have our revenge, General."

"Yes, we will indeed," Garbath replied. "My brother will live to regret what he has done."

"Or not live," Xander added with a frown.

24

It did not take Garbath long to regain his strength. He moved away from his troops and sat alone on the beach, staring out to sea.

Not for the first time, he puzzled at Vadek's change in character and attitude over the past year or so; certainly since Shibboleth had been stolen by the Magars. Garbath had always recognised his brother's burning ambitions, sometimes to the exclusion of developing any warm, personal relationships, and now that Vadek seemed to be frightened of losing his control over the tribe he had become more unapproachable, more indifferent to the views of others. Where he had once ruled as a benevolent, compassionate leader, he now governed in autocratic style. He was suspicious of everyone and everything and had come to rely more and more on the counsel of Panuf. Garbath was convinced that Panuf had poisoned Vadek's mind, having strewn nuggets of misinformation and falsehoods before him. And as a result, Vadek had began to make hasty decisions, such as the use of Time Gates, or his arbitrary demotion of some senior Rathings whom he thought had slighted him in some way. And his refusal to defuse the discord that existed with the Magars, to ignore their past overtures to make peace, had only caused the conflict to escalate. His rejection of Councillor Darma's offer to help retrieve Shibboleth was illustrative of his unreasonable attitude. As a result, an increasing number of tribe members had begun to question who the true ruler was. Was it their Overlord? Or were the strings being pulled by their High Priest? Was Panuf gradually becoming more than the power behind the throne? Was he, in fact, the puppet master?

Garbath's attention was caught by the sight of a French frigate patrolling outside the exclusion zone. Or was it outside the exclusion zone? Garbath very much doubted that. It looked too close. He mentally shrugged off any concern. French, and sometimes Spanish, naval vessels often sailed within British waters, as if to reaffirm their status as enforcers of the blockade and remind the Rathings of their isolation from the rest of the world. And there was absolutely nothing the Rathing government could do. Objections were ignored.

Garbath's troubled thoughts returned to more recent events, and particularly the visit by the supercilious Supreme Council member. All indications pointed to the fact that the Supreme Council was more than casually concerned at the problems taking place at Rumrunner Cove. Garbath knew from his various courtesy visits to other Overlords in the country that none had such problems. He remembered his surprise to learn that they didn't even face any human resistance in their Counties in the form of rebels or freedom fighters. This was put down to the fact that other Rathing Overlords were scrupulously fair to the human populace. Even slave labourers were only tenured for six months every five years, and their living conditions were far better than those provided by Vadek. At Rumrunner, once a human was made a slave he remained so until he died.

And as for the accusations made at the Court hearing, well, those were a pack of lies. Garbath was aware that many Rathings, disillusioned with Vadek's sometime erratic behaviour, had looked to him, Garbath, for alternative leadership decisions, but Garbath had never courted such attention. He thought it grossly unfair to be accused of treachery only because he was a good soldier and popular with his troops as well as many other members of the tribe. Garbath strongly suspected that Panuf was behind all Vadek's accusations. Well, Vadek and his sidekick, the creepy little priest, had thrown down the gauntlet and now Garbath had no option other than to pick it up and fight back. Perhaps, sadly, it is time after all for my brother to be ousted, Garbath thought. He was confident that he'd have the backing of the Supreme Council once this was achieved.

General Garbath rose slowly and made his way back to the encampment. He called his commanders to gather around him.

"War with Vadek is now inevitable. He will soon learn of my escape so he won't be best pleased with events." Garbath looked at his officers and gave a bitter smile. "I wish to make one point clear. My quarrel is with my brother and those hypocrites who surround him with flattery and lies. It is not with the other members of our tribe.

"Regrettably, many on both sides will die in battle. Those of us who assemble here will have done so fighting for truth and justice. I know that what I now ask of you and your troops will not be easy, but I want our opposing force's casualties kept to a minimum. If we are to be successful and I assume the title of Overlord I want to rule over a tribe who bear no grudges towards any of us because of our having inflicted needless slaughter.

"My main objective is to capture Vadek alive. You are to ensure that every single one of your troops knows of this specific instruction. Failure to obey it will result in very severe punishment for the soldier responsible. I want Vadek alive."

25

"What do you mean, no longer there?" Vadek demanded.

The Rathing guard stood nervously to attention. "We were patrolling the beach and when we came to the pylons, there was no sign of General Garbath. The ropes with which he was tied were just lying on the sand, that's all."

"That is all? What do you mean, that is all? Did you search for him?"

The guard's silence was sufficient answer.

"He has probably been rescued by some of his misguided troops," Vadek muttered. He turned to the guard. "Go. Ask Panuf to come and see me."

Vadek paced about his chamber until Panuf entered.

"Overlord," Panuf bowed and saluted in the manner adopted by Rathings.

"Garbath is no longer on the beach," Vadek snarled.

"Escaped?" Panuf queried.

"Saved by his foolish troops, no doubt."

"That is news of great concern. You realise, of course, what he will do next?"

"Of course I do."

Vadek continued to pace about, deep in thought.

He knew that Garbath and his troops would present a formidable force. Much as he appreciated Panuf's counsel, he recognised that any solution to the problem lay with the military. General Rodo, until recently second-in-command to Garbath and now installed as Supreme Commander since Garbath's defection, was the perfect choice to initiate contingency plans. Rodo was familiar with Garbath's thinking. No one knew Garbath's mindset better than General Rodo. Furthermore, Rodo had clearly expressed his disquiet at Garbath's recent behaviour.

"Tell General Rodo to have our Commanders meet here immediately. We must prepare a contingency plan."

Panuf massaged his jaw, deep in thought. He then said, "Garbath controls the elite of our army. If those troops have gone over to his side it will be difficult for us to successfully counter an attack."

Vadek smiled. "Panuf, he must come to us. We have the advantage of our stronghold. Have I ever failed in anything I do?"

"No, Overlord. Your capabilities shine like a beacon in the darkness of night. Your great brilliance is a shining example to all Rathings of your supreme qualities of leadership. We are indeed blessed many times over to have you as Overlord and leader."

"Very well said, Panuf." Vadek tapped his High Priest gently on the shoulder. "You have always had a good appreciation of my outstanding qualities. The action my brother is about to take will be a mere irritation. He and his rebel army will be squashed, annihilated. They are no more than the grains of sand on our beach, to be trampled on."

Panuf put his face between his paws and dry-washed it agitatedly.

"You seem to be overly worried, Panuf?" Vadek said.

Panuf nodded. "This unexpected interruption rather puts paid to our plans for the return of Shibboleth."

"A slight delay only," Vadek smiled.

"What about the boy in the wheelchair? Jago is itching to have him suspended over the wooden stakes he's carefully sharpened."

"A slight delay in that also. We can't have the boy left in the open whilst we engage in teaching my brother a lesson." Vadek stroked his chin in thought. "Keep the boy in solitary. I am sure that once Garbath is defeated the boys on the cliff will return with Shibboleth. If not, then the boy can be given to Jago."

"As you command, Overlord," Panuf bowed. "And may I advance a suggestion?"

"Of course, Panuf."

"I think you should stress to your commanders that you want Garbath captured alive."

"Oh, really? And why?"

"Garbath should be made to pay dearly for his treacherous behaviour. Take him alive. Then summarily execute him before all the tribe. But not in the usual manner. Have him suffer the same fate as that planned for the human boy in the wheelchair."

Vadek gave a perplexed scowl. "You mean impaled on stakes?"

"Precisely. Such an execution would be regarded as an indignity, one hardly fitting for a soldier, a general in the army. It is a form of death meted out to one of little importance. It would set an example to any future rebels. The example would not be lost on the assembled onlookers."

Vadek smiled. "I think you may have a point there."

Panuf bowed. "It will confirm Garbath's stature as being no more than that of a common traitor. His standing will be marked forever with the stain of ignominy. And it would send out a message that you are not to be trifled with. I am confident that such a strong, decisive step would enhance your reputation as a supreme ruler. To an even greater extent than it is now, that is."

Vadek put his arm around the old priest's shoulder and patted him gently. "You have again put forward a very sound idea. Where would I be without you, Panuf?"

Panuf looked up at Vadek. "I only speak out loud the judgements that you have already reached but are far too busy to broadcast. Should I inform Jago of your idea and instruct him to prepare wooden poles of a size suitable to inflict the maximum punishment on Garbath?"

Vadek nodded. "Yes, do so. And I shall tell my commanders to inform their troops of my decision to have Garbath captured alive."

26

Harry Carter sat cross-legged opposite Ashok. "So, what are you doing here, kid?" he asked.

"It's a long story," Ashok replied.

"Yah. Horos told me about it."

"I saw you on the beach last night. You blew up the entrance of one of the caves, didn't you?"

"Yah. My little gang made life a bit more annoying for the Rathings."

Carter had been flown up to the cliff top where he had spent a long time with Horos, Rough Bird and a handful of other Magars. After their talks ended, Carter had walked over to where Ashok sat.

"I hear some of your pals are guests of Vadek," Carter laughed. "He doesn't normally grab kids for slave labour. I guess you must have put him in a right paddy by coming here."

Ashok nodded. "It was a silly thing for us to do."

Carter winked. "So, it's good to buck against conventionality sometimes. Be a free spirit. We all do silly things in life and everything goes pear-shaped. The important thing is to learn from your mistakes, eh? Isn't that right?"

Ashok nodded. "Are you a Yank?" he asked.

"Geez! Purrlease!" Carter exclaimed. "Do me a favour, man."

"Well, you speak funny, like a Yank," Ashok explained.

"No, kid. The accent's South African. Big, big difference. I'm a good old, home-grown and dye-in-the-mud Springbok." Carter laughed again. "Well, I guess we're going to have to do something about this state of affairs."

Ashok gave a puzzled frown and looked hopefully at the man. "You mean help get them out?"

"Yah."

"Hey! That's great!" Ashok said excitedly. "D'you really think you could?"

"Yah."

"Thanks, Mr Carter," Ashok's face was lit with pleasure and a newborn optimism.

"Harry, please." Carter leant back against the rock face and closed his eyes. "Boy! I love the feel of the sun on my face. Summer's the best time, man. Winter's strictly for the birds." He gave another of his unaffected laughs. "Not these guys," he pointed towards the Magars. "This lot are great pals to have around – especially in a tight corner."

Ashok smiled happily. He looked at Carter, noting his deeply suntanned face and arms. Carter looked like a man who enjoyed the open air. What had he said, about bucking against conventionality? I bet he's made an art of it, Ashok thought. Carter was a stocky, muscular man in his early thirties with long black hair and an equally dark beard which was neatly trimmed. He wore faded jeans, an open-neck blue denim shirt and heavy-duty army-style boots. A rifle was slung over one shoulder and a bandolier over another. The red bandana tied at an angle around his head gave him a rather rakish look, so that he almost resembled a pirate one saw in films.

Ashok thought that all the man needed was a cutlass at his waist to complete the picture.

"D'you do a lot of the blowing-up stuff against the Rathings?" Ashok asked.

"A fair bit," Carter replied.

"Have you done this for long?"

"Yah."

"Wouldn't you prefer to escape from here and return to another town where they can't find you?"

"Nope. I enjoy doing this. I've got a great group of guys and gals who also get a helluva kick creating mayhem amongst the Rathings. None of us would swop this life for a boring existence in some far-off town."

Ashok was keen to learn how soon Jack, Bill and Jimmy could be freed. "When d'you think you can save my pals?"

"Not sure at the moment," Carter answered. "I'll have to give it some thought."

Carter studied Ashok. The boy looks tough and capable, Carter thought. His height, build and squiffy nose made him look older than his years. If the lad had arrived here with a view to joining Carter and his band of rebels, Carter would not have hesitated to recruit him. But Carter realised that Ashok was only a kid, despite his outward appearance, and he and his pals had to be rescued somehow.

Ashok wondered if he should ask Carter about the Time Gates that Rough Bird had mentioned. Ever since Rough Bird had told Ashok about them, he had been mulling over the matter and an idea had slowly developed. Ashok had been born when the Rathings already ruled the nation. He was used to them but, like all people, he found it difficult to accept their dominion. He acknowledged the fact that, at most times, the Rathings didn't interfere in the lives of people. But no humans were happy to have them as their rulers and masters. And the occasional raid on homes in order to recruit slave labourers was a constant fear.

Ashok was curious as to how much Carter might know about Time Gates. He looked like the kind of man who'd be bound to know about such things.

"Mr Carter – sorry – Harry. Do you know anything about Time Gates?"

Carter looked at him quizzically. "Sure. But that's an area you want to stay well away from."

"D'you know where any of them are located?"

"Yah. Why d'you want to know, kid?"

"Just curious."

"There's a lot of truth behind the saying 'curiosity killed the cat'. Leave Time Gates well alone, young fella. You don't fool around with Time Gates like you and your pals fooled around by walking through the cave onto this cove."

"Hadn't you ever thought of using a Time Gate to go back and stop the scientist who created these clones?"

Carter shook his head. "Boy, you *do* live in some fantasy world!" Carter exclaimed. The glint of laugher in his dark-brown eyes, ever present, was now replaced by a hard, cold look. "If that's some crazy idea rolling around in your head, forget it. There's no knowing what period in history you're transported to. And unless you know where a return Gate is located, you'd never be able to come back. It's a very dangerous thing, man. Not a game."

Ashok shrugged. "Sorry," he said. "I was just curious."

Carter now smiled. "OK, kid. Just keep your curiosity in check."

He rose and made to shake hands with Ashok. "I've got to be going. Nice meeting you, kid. Keep happy, things could be worse."

"Oh, yes?" Ashok raised his eyebrows in a question mark.

"Yah. You could get lost for ever in a Time Gate. Or you could be dead." Carter saw Ashok's astonished expression. He gave a roaring laugh and patted Ashok on the shoulder. "Just kidding. See ya around." As he walked away he raised his hand in a farewell salute and said in a very affected English accent, "Well, toodle-pip, old son. Must dash."

The South African strolled over towards the Magars. "Where's the down elevator, pals?" he shouted out with another loud laugh. "I've got a date on the beach."

27

Hidden behind the sand dunes at the northern end of the beach, General Garbath and his contingent watched as the labour force finished their day's work and were allowed to bathe in the sea. They heard the guards order the bathers out. Bill and Jimmy, who had been allowed to work in the large tunnel that day so as to be able to make their supposed escape, slipped away from the main body of prisoners and hid behind some rocks. Garbath saw this happen. He and his colleagues thought it unusual for the guards not to notice such an obvious attempt to escape. When everyone had left the beach, the two fugitives ran onto the beach and began calling out and waving wildly at the cliffs. Garbath was not surprised when some fifteen minutes later several Magars landed on the beach and took the two young humans to the cliff top.

Garbath smiled. It was like a game of chess, a game of tit for tat. He wondered what devious plan Vadek had in mind.

On the cliff top, the three boys huddled together, comforted by a collective presence.

Further along the cliff top, Horos and Rough Bird also conferred. But their talk was one of suspicion and concern.

"It all looks too neat, Rough Bird," Horos said quietly. "Something is afoot. Have you ever known the guards not notice any attempted escape?"

"Not that I've ever seen."

"It is as if the two human children were instructed to hail us. They showed no fear of their captors appearing as they shouted out to us. It's all very strange. I suspect the hand of Vadek behind this. It is an act, but played out for whose benefit?"

Rough Bird nodded in agreement.

"Keep an eye on the human children," Horos instructed.

Ashok was able to tell Bill and Jimmy what he knew of the Magars. He told them of his meeting with Harry Carter and how the South African freedom fighter had promised he'd save them all. He also relayed the interesting information that he had gained about the existence of Time Gates.

"Well, it's just Jack he and his men must save," Bill said. "Did he sound sure that he could do it?"

"If anyone can, he can," Ashok replied, then added, "I've also got an idea I want to toss over to you guys."

"OK, spit it out then," Jimmy said.

"When the Rathings were first cloned yonks ago, d'you think the scientist who did it knew that these mutants would eventually rule Britain?"

"Go on," Jimmy said impatiently. "Or is this a history lesson?"

"I know the scientist's name," Bill said.

"So does everyone. His name was Professor Jens Andersen. We were told that at school." Jimmy retorted.

"I wasn't," Bill remarked in a disappointed voice. "Doctor Fournier told me."

"What if we went through a Time Gate and found this professor, hopefully before he started his experiment?" Ashok asked.

"You mean duff him up?" Jimmy smiled at the thought.

Ashok ignored the comment. "If we found him we could explain that the mutant clones he created took over control of the UK. Perhaps we could persuade him to drop the idea."

"Hey, that's pretty cool!" Bill exclaimed.

"That's a pretty load of balls!" Jimmy retorted. "First of all we don't know where the guy lives."

"We could find out," Ashok said.

"And you think a bunch of kids can turn up at his pad and make him believe that we're from the future and have come back to haunt him unless he changes his ideas?" Jimmy laughed. He made quote marks in the air. "Like, brilliant!" he added sarcastically.

"I'm sure we could persuade him once he had the facts," Ashok insisted.

Jimmy shook his head. "OK, genius. Firstly, do you know where we find this Time Gate?"

"No. But I know someone who does."

"Big deal!" Jimmy clapped his hands in mock congratulations. "So we find this Time Gate. It takes us back in time. What time? How far back? How will you feel coming face to face with Julius Caesar who came over here saying 'Veni vidi vici' or whatever he's supposed to have said when he landed? You could arrive in Roman Britain."

"I didn't know you knew Latin," Bill said sarcastically to Jimmy.

"Don't be a smartarse," Jimmy scowled at Bill. "You know what I mean."

"Of course, we'd have to find out more about how

149

these Time Gates work. But I'm sure there's an answer somewhere," Ashok insisted.

Jimmy just grunted.

Bill then explained Vadek's plan to Ashok.

"The tin's empty," Ashok said. "The Magars destroyed the formula."

"It's the formula that Vadek wants. That's what their god left for them." Bill was flustered. How could they possibly return and explain that they didn't have the formula?

"Seriously, mate," Jimmy said despairingly. "You're not really thinking of going along with what that big rat-face plans, are you?"

"We've no choice," Bill said. "He's holding Jack as hostage and we're stymied without the formula."

Jimmy laughed. "And you believe he's going to let us go free once we hand over his tin?"

"We could explain why the formula isn't in it," Bill reasoned.

"With or without any explanation," Jimmy shook his head. "He's never gonna let us go. We're safer here with these bird-thingies."

"Maybe there's a way the Magars can help us, if we tell them what Vadek wants," Ashok suggested.

"No!" Bill exclaimed. "Vadek was definite that we mustn't tell them about the plan."

"Then I don't know what we can do," Ashok shrugged helplessly. "You don't want us to tell the Magars," he said looking at Bill. "And you," he turned towards Jimmy, "feel strongly that we won't get our freedom even if we hand the tin over. And we don't even have the formula. So what's the answer?"

"Hold on and see what this Harry Carter comes up with," Jimmy suggested.

"We've only got three days," Bill said despairingly.

The three boys stayed silent, frustrated by the situation in which they found themselves. Eventually, Bill asked, "What gives with the old man?"

"He's badly hurt," Ashok replied.

"Has he told you anything?"

"Only that he was a prisoner sentenced to death. He was OK at first but was badly injured. He's got worse, fever and wild ramblings of his mind. He's kinda rabbited on about all kinds of things. I'm sure he's now a bit touched up there," Ashok said, patting his head.

"Everyone around here seems to be touched up there," Jimmy said, tapping his own head. "This whole thing's barmy."

The boys stopped talking. There didn't seem to be any answer to the problem they faced.

Jimmy wondered how Jack was managing to move about without having him there to carry him. He doubted the Rathings would let Jack have his wheelchair back.

Bill wasn't sure if the Rathings would move Jack to the main prison cell with Doctor Fournier and the others. He suspected that Vadek would elect to continue to keep Jack in solitary confinement.

They saw Rough Bird walking towards them. "Hello," he said.

"Hey, man!" Ashok turned to both Bill and Jimmy. "This is Rough Bird."

Bill and Jimmy nodded.

"I'm sorry to tell you that the man has just died," Rough Bird announced.

Ashok felt a great sadness at this news. "I'm sorry," he said. "He seemed like a nice person."

Rough Bird nodded. "He got to be quite delirious in the end. From what you said before, he won't be

151

forgotten by his friends. It'll be nice for him to be spoken of."

"Well, I'll certainly remember and speak of him," Ashok confirmed.

"So will we," Rough Bird said as he moved away.

Jimmy nudged Ashok. "So what's all this secret conversation? What's this about what you said before?"

Ashok knew that Jimmy could be annoying and this example was typical of the cocky twerp. "Forget it, man. It's got nothing to do with you."

Jimmy just shrugged and walked away. He was extremely puzzled by Ashok's reaction to his question.

Later Jimmy and Bill, guided by Ashok, took the opportunity to look around the Magar settlement. This was the first opportunity they had of studying these creatures close up. Their earlier, first, encounter on the beach had been somewhat chaotic and remained a blur in their memory.

What seemed like tens of hundreds of these creatures dotted the cliff top as far as the eye could see. There were scores of large domed nests made of loosely woven sticks, in which some Magars were nesting. Others walked or flew around. There was no uniformity in how the nests were placed; they were scattered about in a haphazard manner.

"It must be difficult for them," Bill observed, "as magpies like to roost and nest in trees. But there aren't many of those up here."

"Well, they're not just magpies but half human," Ashok said. "So it shouldn't be that bad for them. But they obviously don't know anything about town-planning. Look at the crazy way their nests are scattered all over the place."

The boys saw several really small Magar babies, slightly smaller than themselves, who looked rather endearing. They exchanged amused glances at how funny the youngsters looked with their small bird heads and torsos atop tiny human legs and feet. The babies were just learning to walk and seemed to favour the hopping movements preferred by magpies and other birds. The three lads noted that whilst the Magars used the human tongue and English language when they spoke to each other, there were occasions when they adopted the raucous chaw-chaw-chaw call typical of magpies. This cacophony of sound was now uppermost, coming mostly from the nesting Magars, whom the boys assumed to be the mothers of the babies. The boys wondered if this was a sign of panic due to the fact that three humans were so close to them. Although what danger three puny humans could pose to the gigantic clones was questionable.

"Boy! This is some sight," Bill said in awe.

"Unbelievable, isn't it?" Ashok agreed.

Jimmy just stood there, mouth open, eyes transfixed on the swarm of these half-bird, half-human creatures. "Cor! There must be thousands in this pack of bird-thingies!"

"A collection of magpies isn't called a pack," Bill corrected Jimmy. "It's either a mischief or a tiding of magpies."

"Blimey! Aren't we a clever one, fat boy?" Jimmy gave a sarcastic smirk. "Listen, sunshine, if I want to call 'em a pack I'll bloomin' well call 'em a pack. You can stick your mischief or glad tidings wherever you fancy, right?"

After a while, Ashok spoke. "Well, what are we going to do?"

"We could smash the tin up, stamp on it and then throw it down to the beach," Jimmy suggested.

"What would that achieve?" Bill asked angrily.

"Jink off the Rathings."

"And what about Jack?" Ashok demanded.

Jimmy sighed and leant back against the rock face. "When are you two going to get it into your thick skulls that there's nothing we or anyone can do about him. He's stuck down there. We're stuck up here." Jimmy didn't feel it necessary to tell Bill and Ashok about Panuf's threatened method of killing Jack if they failed. He had convinced himself that it was no more than a bluff and would not be carried out. He considered his supposed torture by Jago as a similar bluff. True, he'd pretended to have fainted. But why hadn't they come back for him? No, they wouldn't kill Jack, Jimmy surmised. He'd be more use to them kept alive as a slave.

He leant forward and looked earnestly at the other two. "We can't go down there and save him. We can't give the formula to Vadek because we don't 'ave it. So, he won't set us free – you don't 'ave to be a bloomin' genius to know how his mind works. The only chance we have is to talk these bird-thingies into flying us over the cliff top and dropping us off on our beach."

"I can't believe what you're suggesting. You're saying blow our friend and look after ourselves," Ashok snapped.

Jimmy nodded. "That's right, sunshine. Look after *numero uno*. There's no room for heroics in this situation. OK, OK, so I'm sorry for Cripple left down there, but what else do you suggest?"

154

"His name is Jack, not Cripple. I sometimes think you're as sensitive as a dog turd. And I also think you'd better shut up before I thump you one," Ashok was very angry.

Jimmy just laughed and turned to Bill. "And what about you, fat boy?"

"I think you'd better take Ashok's advice," Bill said quietly. "And I've asked you before to stop calling me that."

28

It was deep at night when about a dozen shadowy figures slunk out of the Rathings' cave and crept slowly along the cliff side. They appeared to be carrying something rolled in a blanket or carpet. Whatever it was struggled from time to time. A crescent moon played peekaboo, occasionally glancing shyly from behind wispy dark clouds. The cliff face was black and cold and glared down onto the beach with a sullen expression. The shadowy figures now moved at pace, heading for the northern perimeter of the beach. They rounded the skirt of rocks that led to the Smugglers' Retreat beach. They eventually reached the rebel army's stronghold, where they were challenged by sentries, questioned and detained.

Garbath was sitting in his tent with several of his staff officers when a sentry entered.

"General," he announced. "We have detained thirteen of Vadek's staff, who say they bring you a gift."

"What is this gift?" Garbath was puzzled. "Are they deserters? Or do they come on Vadek's instructions?"

"What they said would indicate that they may be deserters."

"Bring them in." Garbath turned to his officers. "This sounds very odd. A gift?"

Sentries escorted the arrivals who held between them a carpet that struggled violently. They all bowed to Garbath and saluted him by placing their right paw on their left breast. They all wore military uniform.

"Well," Garbath asked, "Explain yourselves."

One of the visitors stepped forward. "I am Captain Sasho. My colleagues and I wish to join your force, General Garbath, and, as a sign of our good faith, we bring you a gift."

Garbath leant forward in his chair and pointed at the struggling carpet. "Is that your gift?"

Captain Sasho nodded. "Allow me to present it to you." With that he stepped forward and pulled one end of the carpet sharply so that it unrolled and spilled its contents. The spluttering figure of Panuf sat in the middle of the unfolded carpet.

"What is the meaning of this?" Garbath shouted angrily.

"We are unhappy with the way things are in our tribe. We kidnapped the High Priest to bring him to you to do as you will with him. Without his influence it is possible that Overlord Vadek will be at some loss to know how to cope with matters. "

Garbath instructed some of his officers to help Panuf up and give him a seat. He then spoke to Panuf. "Have you been hurt?" he asked.

The little priest shook his head. "No. Only my pride."

"Tell me what happened, Panuf?"

"I was asleep when these ruffians burst into my room, bundled me up in that filthy, dusty carpet and brought me here. That is all there is to say, really, about their disgraceful behaviour."

Garbath turned to the group of deserters. He

157

spoke in a low, angry tone. "All of my troops are honourable Rathings. We fight to correct a dishonour done to me. You are officers and crew in the service of the tribe's Overlord. Had you come over to our side with honour you would have been welcomed. But what you have done this night is ignoble. You have attacked a senior member of our tribe and one who is not even military. You have taken hostage a civilian. This is not the military and honourable way to do things. Your action is cowardly, in bad taste and totally unacceptable."

Garbath then addressed Panuf. "Panuf. You have suffered great indignity tonight. My staff will see that you are returned safely to your home." He turned to the deserters. "As for you miserable excuses for Rathings, I give you a choice. If I simply let you walk out, you will have nowhere to go. There is nowhere for you to hide. You will be outcasts and hunted down. You may return to your quarters and face the inevitable punishment that Vadek will mete out or be prepared to die swiftly by sword here."

"General Garbath," Panuf said. "I thank you for your good manners and will gladly accept escort back to my quarters. As for these traitors, I would prefer they be also escorted back so that they may be punished for what they have done."

"I don't doubt that you would prefer that. However, these soldiers came here as volunteers, but their decision to kidnap you was misguided. I am therefore not inclined to accept their services but neither am I disposed to have them tortured because of their foolishness. If they are to die, they should die like soldiers and not humiliated by severe physical and mental pain. As a measure of their worth perhaps we should leave the choice to them." He looked at the deserters. "Well?" he asked. "What is your decision?"

Captain Sasho stood to attention. "I know I speak for all. We prefer an honourable death here."

"A good choice. You have answered bravely."

Garbath walked to the tent entrance and stood at the open flap, looking out at the night sky. He was very conscious that his decision on the fate of the new arrivals was one that would be critically assessed by his troops. In one respect, Garbath was annoyed at Sasho and his companions for having thought that presenting to him the tribe's High Priest as a hostage would cast them in a favourable light. And yet, Garbath recognised that their foolish action was symptomatic of the rashness of youth. To have them killed because of their foolishness would be nothing short of murder. And their summary execution would undoubtedly cause some unrest amongst his troops.

He was aware that all those gathered in the tent were waiting for his ruling.

He turned and walked back into the tent. "I have decided, on reflection, to allow you to join my troops. Your action in taking our High Priest hostage was foolish, but I do not believe that there was any hidden malice behind it. I shall give you, therefore, the opportunity to redeem yourselves in the battle to come. You may all have a soldier's death in the forthcoming battle. You may be fortunate and con-tinue to live a soldier's life." He smiled at Captain Sasho and his companions. "It is all in the hands of God Andersen."

29

Vadek's guards were alerted by the sound of the marching feet of General Garbath's advancing force. Garbath's troops were in full battle uniform. As they did not have any supplies of paint, their dried sea-weed thongs remained uncoloured.

Vadek's troops had painted their seaweed thongs black. Vadek and his officers had painted their corks yellow. Vadek's spear was painted red. He wore his policeman's helmet, which, on this important occasion, was tied around his chin with a red ribbon.

Vadek's army had taken up their usual formation of a large square, shields held protectively around them, spears and lances jutting out.

A phalanx of General Garbath's heavily armed rebel soldiers marched slowly and steadily from the northern perimeter of the beach. They, too, marched in an enormous square, its size taking up most of the beach. Garbath and his Commanders stood at the front. They stopped some hundred metres from the front line of Vadek's soldiers. The opposing armies stood facing each other.

The sun beat down mercilessly. No one moved. No one spoke. They stood still as statues for nearly five minutes, quietly eyeing each other. A deathly silence descended on Rumrunner Cove.

On the cliff top, Ashok, Bill and Jimmy had a panoramic view of the impending battle. The hundreds of opposing giant mutant clones presented a formidable sight. All the Magars, dotted in various cliff-top positions, also watched.

"Would it be too much to hope that they all destroy themselves?" Rough Bird said wistfully.

"I gave up believing in miracles a long time ago," Horos replied and slapped Rough Bird playfully on his shoulder.

General Garbath walked forward a few paces and approached Vadek's contingent.

"Vadek," he called out. "I crave a word with you. Under a flag of truce."

Panuf, standing besides Vadek, whispered. "It could be a trick, Overlord."

Vadek shook his head. "No. Whatever my brother's faults, duplicity is not one of them. That is why he could never become a great leader."

Vadek stepped forward. He walked slowly towards Garbath.

The two Rathings stopped about a couple of metres from each other. Garbath saluted Vadek by placing his right paw against his left breast. He spoke first.

"Brother, I have no desire to fight you or for many of our tribe to die today in battle. But I have been wronged. I have been falsely accused of treason and unjustly sentenced to death. All I want is for you to

161

acknowledge that you made a mistake. And for me to regain my rightful place in the tribe." He leant closer. "If you agree to do this publicly, then we need not embark on this futile battle and its dire consequences."

Vadek was so incensed that he chose to ignore Garbath's words of reconciliation. He looked up at his brother. "Garbath," he stated, "You are neither a General nor my brother. You are no more than a rebel, leading other rebels. How dare you address me as brother? How dare you launch a battle against your Overlord? Do you think that your empty words excuse you? What you do here, arrogantly facing me, is treason. And you say you were falsely accused of treason?" Vadek laughed. "Go on, Garbath. Throw your rebels at me. Then see how they will bite the dust and how you, Garbath, will meet your ultimate fate here on this ground of battle."

Garbath shook his head. "Can I not persuade you to see reason?"

Vadek laughed even louder. "Reason? You call this reason? Advancing with your rebels to confront *me*, your Overlord?"

"May we not take a while to talk? Can we not reach some compromise, if not full agreement?"

"No," Vadek snapped.

"I repeat. This battle is not necessary. What dissension exists should be kept between the two of us. I propose that we resolve matters by single combat."

Vadek scowled. "Are you for one moment suggesting that you and I alone should settle our differences here?"

Garbath shook his head. "No, brother. I do not challenge you to single combat. I am a soldier, a well-trained fighter and you are not. I invite you to choose your best warrior and I will fight him. You have many capable fighters in your ranks. Select one and offer him suitable reward if he fights as your champion."

Vadek stroked his chin and smiled. "Yes, Garbath. I like your idea. And I know exactly who I will appoint. Captain Redif. He is acknowledged as amongst the best. He is young, strong and has proved his worth in many a battle."

"An excellent choice," Garbath agreed. "Let him be your champion. He and I will fight until one of us is beaten."

"A fight to the death!" Vadek said.

"That is not what I had in mind," Garbath shook his head. "The side of the one who loses will accept the other's decision. But death is quite unnecessary."

"No. If it is to be single combat then it is to be to the death," Vadek insisted.

Garbath nodded. "Your desire to see blood spilt saddens me. Should Captain Redif win will you then agree that there will be no battle?"

Vadek nodded.

"And if I were to defeat Redif, do you agree that my troops will not be punished and that I shall be exonerated and all charges will be dropped?"

Again Vadek nodded.

"Then I challenge your champion to battle," Garbath stated abruptly.

"Very well, Garbath," Vadek smiled. "I accept your challenge. Single combat to the death."

"May God Andersen look down kindly on us this day," General Garbath said.

Vadek nodded. "All blessings to God Andersen and to the safe return of Shibboleth."

The two brothers turned away from each other and made their way back to their respective troops.

30

Jack was carried to the torture chamber by a Rathing guard.

Jago was waiting for him. He told the boy to stand on a rather ancient set of bathroom scales and made a note of Jack's weight. He then made further jottings of Jack's height.

Jack watched the Rathing's Chief Torturer and Executioner rummaging about in a corner of the chamber. Jago appeared to be enjoying his task. He kept humming a somewhat odd, dirge-like tune as he continued to search for something.

"Aha! Just the thing," he exclaimed, holding up a coil of fairly thick rope He moved towards Jack and told him to hold his arms upwards.

"We must be sure that the length and thickness of the cord is suitable to bear your weight and yet fray on burning within the time limit I have been given," he explained as he experimentally tied the rope around Jack's wrist. "If I am to suspend you for three days I don't want your arms popping out of their sockets, do I?" He grinned.

Jack felt sick. He tried very hard to control his breathing so as not to go into a panic attack.

"I thought you were going to put me in a cage. Are you going to hang me by my wrists?" he asked.

Jago nodded.

"For three days?"

Jago nodded again.

"I think I'll be dead before the three days are up," Jack said quietly. "My arms couldn't bear my weight for such a long time."

Jago grinned again. "You can be sure that you would live for three days, human, the way I'd tie you. But, I will be making some adjustments. For example, you will be supported from time to time by planks of wood which I shall place under your feet," Jago explained. "That is when we give you water to drink. You will have no food during that time, but water will be essential as I want you to be fully conscious when you fall to your death." Jago beckoned Jack forward. "Come. Let me show you my handiwork."

He guided Jack towards one of the far corners of the cell. "There are your instruments of death," Jago said proudly, pointing to about half a dozen wooden stakes placed against the wall. "They will be waiting underneath you." He took hold of one of the posts and held it out towards Jack. "Feel the sharpness of the point," he invited. "Is that not a work of art?"

Jack didn't touch the sharpened pole and said nothing. He was feeling weak and asked if he could sit down on the floor.

Jago nodded. "I have finished with you." He signalled to a guard. "Take him away now."

31

Captain Redif walked slowly past his companions and made his way towards the centre ground between the two opposing armies.

He carried a shield across his back, a spear in one paw and an unsheathed longsword in the other.

Redif was a huge Rathing, even bigger than Garbath, and his jet-black fur glistened with the oil that he had liberally rubbed all over his body. As a highly experienced fighter, he knew that the oil would make it difficult for his opponent to retain any hold should their fight involve close contact grappling. Redif was aware of Garbath's legendary strength and fighting skills, but he was confident that his youth and fitness could overcome his older opponent. He concluded that in order to gain some advantage over his more experienced foe he would have to launch a surprise assault. Attack swiftly before he expects it, Redif said to himself. Attack is the best form of defence.

General Garbath already stood alone on the beach, his arms folded across his chest. At his waist was a sheathed longsword, the double-edged "knight's" sword much favoured by Rathings because of its length and weight. He carried no other weapons or shield. He waited patiently for Redif to reach him.

Redif stopped within a metre of Garbath. He tapped his left breast with his right paw.

"I salute you, General Garbath."

"I salute you, Captain Redif."

"I respect you, General," Redif said. "I come to face you as ordered by our Overlord Vadek. I have no quarrel with you, General, but I must do my duty as commanded."

Garbath nodded. He had noticed the thick coating of oil on Redif's fur and smiled at the younger Rathing's preparations. "May the best Rathing win."

"I have been instructed by my Overlord that we must fight to the death."

"Such is his wish," Garbath replied bluntly.

"May God Andersen look kindly on us and grant he who is to die a swift and clean death," Redif said.

Garbath gave a kind, friendly smile to the younger soldier. "Shall battle commence?" he began to ask, but Redif was already rushing at him with sword raised.

Garbath was taken by surprise and was obliged to take several paces backwards in order to give himself time to unsheath his own sword. In doing so, he stumbled in the sand and came crashing down.

Redif brought his sword arm down, slashing at the sprawled figure of Garbath. Redif's sword cut through Garbath's tunic and drew blood.

Garbath wrapped one leg around Redif's right leg and pushed hard against Redif's thigh with the other foot.

Redif fell backwards.

This gave Garbath the few seconds he needed in which to scramble to his feet. Garbath moved back to allow the younger Rathing time to get up.

Redif once again rushed forward, striking at Garbath, who parried the attack with his sword.

Redif hit out at Garbath with his shield, smashing it into Garbath's unprotected shoulder. Garbath felt his muscles knot in pain, but he stood firm, giving no indication that the force of the blow had numbed his shoulder.

The two warriors moved around each other. Redif kept stabbing out, searching for an opening, and testing Garbath's reflexes.

Garbath remained out of weapon distance, constantly feinting to his left and his right. He could sense the frustration of the younger soldier in being unable to find his target.

On the cliff top, Magars and the boys observed the dance of death taking place on the beach. On either side of the circling warriors, both armies stood and also watched.

Panuf leant towards Vadek and whispered, "I rather think that Captain Redif might have the measure of Garbath. Garbath keeps moving back, as if unsure or afraid."

Vadek said nothing but nodded, his eyes never leaving the two combatants.

"The terms agreed with Garbath is that if Redif wins, Garbath's rebels lay down their arms, is that so?"

Again Vadek nodded.

"And should Garbath win? Is he forgiven his sins and we do not make him and his rebels account for their treachery?"

"Should Garbath not die at Redif's paws, then he

will die in the battle to follow," Vadek said quietly, as if to himself.

"Was that the agreement?" Panuf sounded surprised.

"I do not make agreements with rebels," Vadek replied, turning away from the scene on the beach and looking directly at Panuf. "Single combat was Garbath's idea. He can die either one way or the other."

Panuf smiled up at his Overlord. "I admire your cunning, Overlord."

Vadek smiled back. "Garbath has not the guile to outwit me. He will die on this sand today, of that there is no doubt."

In his frustration at not being able to come close to his opponent, Redif raised his spear and launched it at Garbath. Garbath sidestepped, but a little too late and a little too slow. The spear pierced his left shoulder. The wound was not deep as the shaft drooped downwards. Garbath reached for it with his right paw and yanked it out. At the same time, Redif rushed forward and slashed at Garbath with his sword. As Garbath parried, Redif stepped up to the older Rathing and wrapped his arms around Garbath's arms, pinning them against Garbath's sides.

The pain in Garbath's injured shoulder was excruciating but he refused to cry out. He struggled to free himself.

Redif's decision to oil himself now worked against him. His arms could find no firm purchase and they kept slipping down. Redif clasped his right paw over his left wrist and tried hard to maintain his grip, but to no avail.

With an almighty effort, Garbath pushed both his arms upwards and released himself from the tenuous grasp. At the same time, he brought the flat side of his sword blade crashing down against Redif's shoulder.

Redif collapsed from the force of the blow. He was puzzled as to why the General had not hit him with the sharp edge; such a cut would have seriously disabled him.

Garbath then hit Redif on the head with the pommel of the sword. Blood poured from the younger Rathing's smashed skull. Redif was stunned and unable to rise.

Garbath held the point of his sword at Redif's throat. "You have fought well, Captain Redif," Garbath remarked. "I think we might conclude that you are defeated, would you not agree?"

Redif nodded. He closed his eyes, waiting for the sword point to enter his throat. But nothing happened. He opened his eyes to see General Garbath walking slowly away.

"To the death, General!" Redif croaked. "The agreement was that we fight to the death."

Garbath stopped and turned round to face the fallen soldier. "That was Overlord Vadek's condition. Not mine."

Redif hauled himself to his knees. He knelt in the sand and pleaded with his victor. "General, I will be dishonoured if you win and I do not die. Kill me now."

General Garbath returned to where Redif knelt. He gave him his paw and raised him to his feet.

A loud cheer rose from both armies.

"Do not seek death so eagerly, Captain Redif. You have fought well and bravely. You have no reason to feel dishonoured." Garbath raised his sword in front

170

of his face in a salute to Redif. "If my suspicions are right, I believe that Overlord Vadek will decide that there will be a battle after all. As I have not met his condition of combat to death, he will find this a perfectly excusable reason to not agree to the other terms. You will have plenty of opportunity to face death here today. May God Andersen look on you favourably, Captain Redif. Now go. Return to your troops and to your leader."

With that, Garbath walked away towards his troops.

A savage, horrific and brutal battle of opposing giant mutant clones was about to commence.

32

Vadek's main force advanced in their usual formation, shields ready to be held above their heads and around their sides. Each force carried several banners displaying their "colours". These large banners, vertical and oblong in shape, served as a rallying point during the course of battle. Vadek's troops carried several banners, all of which bore the same design, namely a white background with black crescents. They marched forward, slow and ponderous, seemingly impregnable.

Behind Vadek's advancing square were other soldiers who carried no shields but had several dozen spears held in quivers over their shoulders. To the rear, obscured by the giant Rathings, were hordes of Droons. They scurried along in their usual haphazard manner, waiting for the order to use their slingshots.

Garbath, his injured shoulder roughly bandaged, was not surprised that Vadek had not stood down his troops. He turned to his officers who were gathered around him. "As I suspected, it appears that Overlord Vadek has decided not to honour the agreed terms of single combat. It is no doubt because Captain Redif still lives. Order the advance."

Garbath's square now split into three parallel columns. The first column was made up of Commander

Xander's 1st Corps. His banners were black with deep-red short vertical stripes. Commander Mordon and his 3rd Corps headed the middle column and proudly displayed their banners of red background with green squares. Commander Kera and her 2nd Corps of female Rathings formed the right column. Their banners had a light-blue background with four yellow dots. The female Rathings who made up the 2nd Corps were renowned as the bravest and fiercest of all the army divisions.

The boys crouched on the cliff-top edge and watched the two advancing armies. The many hundreds of marching feet caused the ground to tremble, as if terrified at the carnage about to be unleashed upon it. The engagement was going to be hard and bloody, and no Rathing would be prepared to give ground to another unless sword or spear cut him down.

"Wow!" Bill exclaimed. "This is going to be one big battle."

"And we've got ringside seats," Jimmy laughed. He turned to Ashok and jokingly said, "Pass the popcorn and Pepsi, will you mate?"

Vadek had expected both armies to clash head on, square to square. But Garbath's unusual troop formation perplexed Vadek. As Garbath's troops drew near, the two outer columns peeled off to the left and to the right respectively of the battlefield, leaving the centre column – Commander Mordon's 3rd Corps – to face the full might of Vadek's square formation.

This move surprised Vadek. They had never

adopted such a tactic in their major battles against the Magars. Vadek's troops began to slow down, uncertain how to deal with such an unexpected move.

The two outside columns marched steadily on a forward angle, away from the main battleground.

Vadek, Panuf and some of Vadek's senior Commanders now stood at the rear of their troops, ready to direct the battle. Panuf turned to Vadek. "Look! He's lost any advantage of brute strength in a clash with our soldiers. Why, he's moved two columns away from the main thrust of our army. Madness!" Panuf shrieked and jumped up and down with unrestrained glee. "One corps to attack our army! They'll be annihilated! Oh joy! Oh joy!"

Vadek ignored Panuf. He turned to General Rodo. "What d'you think he is planning?"

Rodo thought for a moment. "I don't know, Overlord. I am at a loss to explain what General Garbath has in mind."

Then spear-carriers stationed behind Commander Mordon's force launched their weapons. There was complete mayhem amongst Vadek's soldiers as hundreds and hundreds of spears rained down on them. But the havoc caused was not due solely to the spears but to what was attached to them – blazing rags. The spears, all afire, landed on the shields that Vadek's soldiers held above their heads. A fire blazing away over one's head is frightening at any time. Many soldiers broke rank in order to extinguish the flames.

And whilst confusion reigned, Commander Mordon's 3rd Corps suddenly launched their attack. The earth shook and the air thundered with the stamping feet of hundreds of gigantic Rathing soldiers rushing forward.

174

But Rodo was not looking at the attacking force. Instead he kept a watchful, suspicious eye on the two flank columns. They were now at some distance from, but precisely opposite, the two sides of Vadek's infantry square. Both columns had now stopped and turned to face Vadek's force.

Vadek jumped up and down in a furious rage. "This is too much! This is too much!" he shouted. He continued to leap about and had to keep adjusting his helmet that kept falling over his eyes. "He is not conducting a fair fight. I have never seen anything like this in all my battles. Playing with fire on a battlefield! I ask you! The fellow's a maniac!"

General Rodo shook his head in amazement. "Brilliant! Why had I not thought of such a tactic before?"

"Brilliant? Tactic?" Vadek snarled. "You praise the enemy? What's so brilliant about it? He's playing dirty, that's what he's doing. But his one corps against my square will be smashed to smithereens."

"Don't you see, Overlord? General Garbath plans to charge us from the sides as well as the feint of the head-on attack. See, Commander Mordon's forward force have slowed down, but look to the sides!" Rodo pointed to the left and right flanks of Vadek's infantry square. Vadek's troops were so intent on watching and countering the frontal attack and trying to extinguish the burning spears that they were oblivious of the enemy troops now rushing at them on either side.

"He can't do that!" Vadek exploded. "It's against all the rules of warfare! The square! The square! He must attack in square formation! What *is* that mad rat doing?"

Rodo signalled to one of his officers. "Get down there and tell the brigade commanders to have their troops fall back and divide themselves into three squares to counter the three attacking columns. Stress upon them the need to stand firm."

The signals officer ran towards the troops and spoke to one of the officers in charge.

"What are you doing? What are you doing?" Vadek demanded.

"Trying to counter Garbath's move," Rodo explained.

Vadek banged his spear shaft onto the sand and shouted angrily. "Refer to me first, Rodo. I am commander-in-chief. I give the orders."

"Overlord Vadek, it would have taken up too much time if I explained it all to you. It would have been too late to counter Garbath's plan."

Vadek said nothing but looked peeved.

The two armies were getting very close by now. They would strike at each other within minutes.

General Garbath turned to his adjutant, Major Eylau, who stood next to him. "Eylau, they have seen through our plan. I rather think General Rodo has learnt well from our games of chess together. I admire his countermove. Order the rear force to attack immediately."

And so the next surprise presented itself to Vadek and his group of commanders. Approaching at a run from the land side of the beach were more of Garbath's troops, lightly armed with flaming spears. They had been lying down behind some of the dunes, remaining very still and waiting for the order to charge. Others, on the beach side and placed behind some of the cliffs, similarly lightly armed, also dashed into view and began running along the shore-line. Both groups were moving very fast towards the rear of Vadek's troops.

Vadek now faced a forward arrowhead of troops and two claws of Garbath's flank columns as well as advancing fire-carrying spear-troops to his rear. Vadek's army was caught in an encircling pincer movement; and it was too late to take evasive action.

"What is he doing? What is he doing?" Vadek screamed. "You don't fight battles like that! He IS mad! I knew I couldn't trust him!" He turned to Rodo. "Rodo, get a message to Garbath – I don't care how you do it – but tell him he cannot fight like this." Vadek stamped up and down on the sand like a petulant child. The helmet, having fallen over his eyes for the umpteenth time, was discarded with an oath.

Rodo looked quizzically at his leader but did not reply. He realised, not for the first time, that the tribal Overlord sometimes spoke absolute rubbish. He looked down at the sand. He had never seen such tactics deployed and, as an experienced warrior, he secretly admired Garbath's military genius.

The opposing armies clashed loudly, the force of shield against shield. Short sword stabs pierced deep. Spears were thrust hard into opponents. Blood spouted and ran in deep-red rivulets onto the burn-ing sand. Loud piercing screams of anger and pain echoed all around the cove. Giant mutant clone fought giant mutant clone, brother against brother, father against son, tribal kith against tribal kin. The beach shook with a thunderous rolling reverberation each time a mortally wounded giant came crashing down to the ground.

At one stage, Rodo realised that as Xander's 1st Corps advanced, approaching slightly at an angle, they had inadvertently left their right flank exposed. Rodo exploited this mistake by Xander and launched a deadly attack. The fighting was bloody and brutal and Rodo's troops were gradually pushing back Xander's exhausted soldiers.

But Kera's female warriors were unstoppable. They slashed and stabbed their way through to the centre of Vadek's force. Squealing excitedly at the top of their voices, they were like wild, drug-crazed Amazons, impervious to pain, deliriously happy at the sight of enemy blood. It needed more than a dozen sword or spear stabs before one of them could be stopped. Kera stood in the front line and urged her troops on. She held up the decapitated head of an enemy Rathing and waved it around for all to see. "Kill! Kill! Kill!" she squeaked at the top of her voice. "Kill! Kill! Kill!" her troops called back.

On the cliff top, the boys continued to watch in awe at the chequered board of battle taking place below them. They held their breath, fascinated at the sight of such fierce, such ferocious, such bloody close-contact fighting. The deafening noise must have sounded for miles around.

Further along the cliff, Horos, Rough Bird and six other Magars were deep in conversation.

Ashok and Bill looked at each other and Bill said, "What d'you think they're talking about?"

"Search me," Ashok replied. "But I'd say they're planning something."

The Magars broke away from their discussions and walked off in different directions. Each began to signal to other Magars to gather around them.

"Are you thinking what I'm thinking?" Bill said.

Ashok nodded.

Eight separate groups now huddled together like a number of rugby teams holding a pep talk prior to kick-off. After a minute or so they all split and rushed towards mounds of boulders that were dotted all over the plateau.

Jimmy shuffled over towards Ashok and Bill. "Hey!" he exclaimed. "I think these bird-thingies are planning to join in the fun."

"I reckon," Ashok nodded.

"Right on!" Jimmy exclaimed excitedly.

Horos walked past the boys and gently patted them on their heads with his wing. "I thought it a good idea for us to attack the Rathings whilst they are busy killing off each other. We've never had the chance to hit them when they're preoccupied. They make excellent targets in their present state of disarray."

Several groups of Magars now launched themselves from the cliff top. They propelled themselves through the air with one wing, while clutching a boulder with the other; some also carried a boulder between their thighs. They swooped down towards the warring Rathings and began their attack. The Magars stayed well out of range to avoid being hit by any spears. This inevitably meant that they were not always able to find their target. Nevertheless, as many a Rathing was forced to look up so as to avoid

179

being hit, this invariably caused him to let his guard down and an opposing Rathing was able to strike a mortal blow.

As the lifeblood ran from dead and dying Rathings, the rivulets, scarlet red at first, gradually turned black as the burning sand absorbed the spilt blood and gore.

Vadek, who had by now joined his troops on the battlefield, was suddenly aware that no rebel soldier had tried to cut him down. As he cut and thrust at the enemy, he had to parry only half-hearted attempts to stab him. He had at first thought that this was because the rebel soldiers still held him in some esteem as their Overlord. Then the true reason dawned on him. Garbath had obviously issued instructions that he was not to be harmed. Why? What was Garbath's game? Why leave him untouched?

But one thing was obvious. Much as Vadek and Garbath were at odds with each other, neither brother made any attempt to confront the other. In fact, they studiously avoided facing each other, not because of any cowardice, but rather because neither wanted to be the killer of his brother. Other Rathing brothers fought each other. But not Vadek and Garbath.

Vadek turned around, seeking a glimpse of Panuf, but Panuf had run back to hide in the Temple.

There was chaos on the beach. It was at that moment that Horos decided to take further advantage of the situation. He turned to one of his commanders, Argon, and issued an order. "Take some hand-picked helpers and see if you can gain entry into the caves. Try to release the prisoners. This is an excellent moment to save the humans." He gave a vindictive cackle. "That should *really* make Vadek furious!"

He then turned to the boys. "We're going to take you down to the cave entrance. You can make your way home from there. Perhaps this is the opportunity we need. There's so much distraction down there at the moment that I think now is the best chance you've got to try and escape. I can't guarantee it will be successful, but are you willing to try?"

They nodded their heads energetically in agreement.

Horos looked at Argon and gave instructions to proceed.

33

The mayhem on the beach enabled the Magars to fly down and enter the unguarded tunnels leading to the prison cells.

In view of the pending battle, the prisoners had been kept locked up. They were surprised to see a number of Magars rushing down to the tunnel and, after some initial difficulty, unlock the doors of the many cells.

"Go! Go!" the Magars shouted at them. "The Rathings are fighting each other. Go! Escape!"

The two hundred or so prisoners poured out of their cells. Some of them ran along the tunnel straight ahead of them and leading to the beach close to Smugglers' Retreat. They stopped, stunned at the sight before them. There was complete carnage. Hundreds of Rathings and Magars lay dead or dying on the beach. The sand was stained a brilliant scarlet. Savage fighting continued, accompanied by high ratlike squeaks of pain and anger and the excited chaw-chaw-chaw calls of the many hundreds of Magars whose dark plumage blotted out the sky. The battle of the giants presented an awesome spectacle.

To make their escape towards the cave leading to Rumrunner Beach meant they had to traverse along the whole stretch of the beach. Even though they kept close to the cliff side they stood little chance. A few Rathings, seeing the humans running in full view along the beach, threw their spears with deadly accuracy. Death was instantaneous.

Doctor Fournier knew that the tunnel from the prison cells led directly to the beach furthest from where they wanted to exit. He shepherded the rest of the prisoners along the tunnels inside the cave network. He had no doubt that the others, over-anxious in their anxiety to escape, had embarked on a certain suicide mission. Fournier's group made their way inside the cave, past the Temple. They then turned left where the stores and workshops were located. This route took them to an exit point close to the cave entrance leading to Rumrunner Beach.

Fournier instructed his group to creep the short way along the cliff side and away from the battle-ground. They moved slowly and quietly, although any noise they may have inadvertently made would have been lost in the screams of the warring Rathings.

Fournier, who was bringing up the rear of the escapees, growled urgently. "Keep going, keep going. Keep together now."

He saw several Magars land at the cave entrance. They each held Bill, Ashok and Jimmy under one of their wings and dropped them gently onto the sand.

At the same time, a Rathing noticed what was happening. He broke away from the main body of the battle and ran towards the cave entrance.

"Watch out!" Jimmy yelled.

Rough Bird, on hearing Jimmy's warning, turned

to see the Rathing draw back his arm and throw his spear with considerable force. The missile was on a straight course towards Ashok.

Without a moment's hesitation, Rough Bird placed himself in front of Ashok.

The spear went right through his body and he fell to the ground, mortally wounded. He clutched at the shaft of the spear that protruded from his body. Disjointed thoughts scrambled about in his mind, overriding the intense pain. He recalled the face of his mother nursing him as a youngster when he was ill and of his father, teaching him how to build up his strength and how to engage in aerial combat. He thought of his Magar friends, especially those who had died in battle or after extreme torture inflicted by the Rathings. Tiny tears welled in his eyes. And those who stood around him in shock might have thought the tears were due to the pain. But the tears Rough Bird shed were for his distress at the hatred around him. Despite the impression he conveyed as being a tough warrior, concerned only with fighting, Rough Bird had always wished that life could have been pure and simple and pleasurable. He had never been able to reconcile himself with the fact that the Magars and Rathings could not live and play together innocently. And so he wept for the unfairness of life.

Rough Bird looked up at Ashok with pain-filled eyes. "Toodle-pip," he croaked. Then the searing pain lessened and Rough Bird died, his head gently cradled in Ashok's lap. Ashok stroked the big bird's head feathers and whispered, "Toodle-pip, Rough Bird." But the Magar's eyes stared lifelessly at him. Ashok knew that Rough Bird was dead. He passed the palm of his hand across the dead Magar's open eyes and gently closed them. He somehow felt that

184

Rough Bird's belief he would be spoken of and remembered after his death was true. Ashok sensed the pinpricks of held-back tears as he looked down at the giant creature who had been so kind to him on the cliff top.

34

Bill and Jimmy scanned the beach. There was no sign of Jack. Had the Magars set him free? Or had he been overlooked, perhaps locked in a small cell elsewhere in the labyrinth of tunnels?

Ashok moved away from the dead Magar, looked around, and cried out, "Where's Jack?"

"Go! Enter the cave," Fournier shouted to the fugitives and continued to hurry them in. He pushed Ashok's shoulder. "Come on, *mon ami*. It's too dangerous to go back and look for your friend. We must go through the cave."

Ashok struggled, refusing to enter. He turned to see Bill dashing through the cave with the other prisoners.

"Bill!" Ashok shouted after him. "We've got to get Jack."

Bill turned. He was unsure what to do. In some ways he wanted to get as far away as he could from the cove of the vile Rathings. He was frightened of being recaptured and forced again into hard labour. The welcoming arms of freedom beckoned, inviting him to release himself from a life of slavery. Yet, the bond of comradeship was stronger than any casual invitation, no matter how tempting. Bill stood for a few seconds biting his nails, trying to make his mind up. Ashok dashed away from the cave, having made a spur-of-the-moment decision to go back and try and find Jack. Bill hesitated. The temptation of making a getaway was too great. But deserting one's friends could never be condoned. Bill turned and followed Ashok.

Ashok hurried along the beach, making sure he stayed close to the cliff so that the Rathings would not spot him. He reached one of the entrances to the Rathings' tunnels. The sound of running footsteps behind him caused him to stop and spin round in fear. He was petrified, expecting to see a Rathing coming after him. He breathed a sigh of relief when he saw the tubby figure of a somewhat red-faced and sweating Bill.

"Phew! I thought you were a Rathing."

Bill came up to him. He was panting and scared witless. "Come on," Bill said urgently. "Let's keep moving."

They entered the cave, turned left and ran along the corridors. They passed several large cells, all empty, and a number of other cages on one side of the long tunnel. The first one contained sacks of wheat and other foodstuff, most of it spilt on the floor. A further cage was a workshop of some kind. No prison cell. No Jack. The boys quickly retraced their steps. They turned down the next tunnel and dashed up to the end of it. All they passed was rock face. No prison cells. Bill was about to turn left but Ashok stopped him. "That leads to the tunnel we went up before," Ashok shouted, "This way." He was pointing at the tunnel they'd just travelled through.

"We've come up there," Bill pointed out.

"I know, but I think I saw an alcove or something

like that. Let's have a quick look there." Ashok gestured urgently.

They dashed back. As they neared the entrance Ashok noted the small alcove that he thought he had seen. "This way," he called out to Bill. They crept into it and found a high, narrow tunnel leading off to their left. Ahead of them was a small cell. An agitated Jack was locked in it.

"Come on!" Ashok shouted as he dashed forward, "We're getting you out."

"The keys are on a ring on the wall," Jack yelled back.

Ashok looked up and saw the keys. They were placed at an ideal height for a Rathing but far too high for him to reach. He leapt up several times, trying to grab the key ring, but was unsuccessful.

"I can't get to them," Ashok panted.

"Here," Jack instructed. "I'll put my hands through the bars and you step on them and I'll lift you up."

Jack placed his elbows on the rock floor and extended his forearms outside the cell bars.

Ashok hesitated.

"Go on," Jack commanded. "Stand on my hands and I'll raise you. Pull yourself up on the cage bars at the same time to help. Bill, for heaven's sake, don't just stand there like a dummy. Give Ash a hand and push him upwards."

"I'll be too heavy for you, man," Ashok protested.

"Don't argue with me," Jack growled. "I may have to use a wheelchair but I'm not completely useless. Go on, step on my hands," he ordered firmly. "Quick! Quick!"

Ashok put his feet tentatively on Jack's outstretched palms.

"For crying out loud!" Jack shouted. "Stand on

188

them properly, not on tiptoe. You're not a blooming ballet dancer!"

Ashok gave a nervous laugh and took two decisive steps forward. Jack began to raise his arms slowly and with great difficulty. Suddenly he dropped his forearms and swore. "Ouch!" he cried out. The pain on his elbows, pressed hard against the rock floor, was too great to bear. He quickly tore off his T-shirt. He then rolled it up like a sausage and placed it on the cell floor. He settled his elbows on the shirt.

Ashok tried again. Jack's face was twisted from the effort of bearing Ashok's weight. His neck muscles knotted and bulged from the exertion, sweat began to form on his forehead. His heart was pumping loudly with excitement, fear and hope.

Ashok felt himself being raised slowly by Jack and Bill, who had now placed his shoulders beneath Ashok's bottom and began to push. Ashok grasped the cell's metal bars and hauled himself upwards.

"Got 'em!" He yelled as he grabbed the key ring and yanked it off the wall nail. He jumped off Jack's hands.

"Hurry!" Bill shouted. "Hurry!"

"Seriously, Ashok," Jack wheezed. "You're heavier than I thought." His elbows were cut and bleeding, despite the cushioning of the cloth.

Ashok quickly unlocked the cell door. He bent down and lifted Jack, slinging him over his shoulders in a fireman's lift.

"Let's go," he shouted and hurried along the tunnel. Bill stumbled behind. They had reached the exit.

Several Rathing soldiers blocked it.

35

The battle was gradually coming to an end. Neither side had achieved a victory or gained the upper hand. The interference of the Magars by attacking the warring Rathings had swung the odds slightly in Vadek's favour. Garbath's tactical advantage was nullified, and he was extremely surprised that his elite troops, even though fewer than Vadek's, had not gained an outright victory. The last thing Garbath had wanted was a protracted state of hostilities. A stalemate situation had been reached.

Both armies began to withdraw. Garbath led his rebel troops to the northern part of the beach and on to Smugglers' Retreat. Vadek and his soldiers moved back towards their cave. Vadek was furious that he had not totally eliminated Garbath's rebel force.

A few minutes later Vadek watched coldly as a group of soldiers walked towards him, escorting the three boys.

"What have we here?" Vadek asked, and added sarcastically, "I'm afraid you're a little too late to join in the battle."

"We found them trying to escape," one of the soldiers explained.

Vadek nodded. "Put them back in the cell," he said in a resigned voice. "I have other, more pressing, matters to consider. We shall deal with them later."

He then saw Panuf hurrying towards him.

"Ah, Panuf. I didn't see you on the field of battle. You seemed to have left very suddenly."

Panuf gave him a sheepish, gnomelike grin. "Overlord, I was in the Temple invoking God Andersen to give us victory."

Vadek smiled back. "Ever the religious one! Well, God Andersen must have been listening with half an ear. He did not grant us victory. But then neither did he shame us with defeat. Perhaps Garbath prayed to him too? Maybe our god was a bit torn as to which of us he should support? Is it even possible that he didn't really care one way or the other? Tell me, Panuf, what do you think?"

Panuf could not believe he had heard Vadek's expressed sarcasm about God Andersen. He had carefully nurtured Vadek's religious training and believed that Vadek had always been a willing and able pupil. He now wondered if Vadek's past professed blind faith was nothing more than pretence. Perhaps to Vadek, the possession of Shibboleth was merely a very useful tool of control.

Panuf said nothing. Everything he had believed in, the orderly nature of things, seemed to be crashing around him. Panuf felt distraught. He had failed in his mission.

He bowed and departed to pray for the soul of his misguided leader.

36

Jimmy saw Ashok dash out of the escape cave. He knew that Ashok had done so in the hope of rescuing Jack. He then saw Bill stumbling behind Ashok. Jimmy looked back at the rest of the stragglers making their escape. He was tempted to join them. A niggling guilt held him back. He couldn't just leave the three kids on their own. It wasn't right. Jimmy reached a sudden decision and followed Ashok and Bill. The two boys were already some distance ahead and entering the cave leading to the Rathings' quarters. Jimmy hid behind a cluster of large boulders and studied the lie of the land.

His throat was dry from fear and he could hear his heart beating wildly. He took several deep breaths and tried to control his anxiety. He noticed that the battle had ended. He remained hidden for several long minutes, not sure what his next step should be.

Despite his earlier claim on the cliff top, when he told Ashok and Bill that the best philosophy in life was to look after *numero uno*, he realised that in a situation like this watching out for number one wasn't right. His earlier protestations were all a part of his macho image, of his street cred. Street credibility, he now realised, counted for nothing out here.

Then he saw Bill and Jack being carried by Ashok.

They were being led out of the cave entrance by several Rathings and escorted to Vadek, who stood on the beach with some of his officers. Jimmy was too far away to hear what was being said but it was obvious from the gestures and body language that the three kids were to be escorted back into the Rathings' cave. They were to remain prisoners.

The heat of the afternoon sun had lessened in its intensity and the cliff's shadows were beginning to lengthen across the beach. Several Rathings, accompanied by a host of Droons, were gathering the dead and dying and carrying them into the cave. Soon all that remained were some weapons and the bodies of fallen Magars – who, Jimmy presumed, would be collected later by their colleagues. A black ink stain of drying blood on the sand surrounded various body parts. He stared in horror at the dis-membered bodies, gagged and was violently sick. The sight of his puke made him want to be sick again. He covered his vomit with some sand. Jimmy wiped his mouth with his forearm and sat down behind the boulders. When his heaving stomach had calmed down, he thought about the plight of the three other boys. Jimmy was determined to rescue them. But how? He knew that he could not manage it on his own and that he would need help.

Jimmy heard a faint whistle. He glanced around, trying to find out from where it came. He heard it again. Then he saw a red bandana slowly appear from behind a boulder, followed by the grinning face of a dark-haired man with a black beard. The man put his fingers to his lips, indicating silence. With his other hand, he indicated that Jimmy should keep down. The man and the boy remained still as stat-ues, each hiding behind a boulder. After a couple of minutes, the man crawled on his stomach towards Jimmy.

He gave Jimmy another wide grin. "Pardon me, sir," he said in an odd accent. "Are you with the Azalea Tours group visiting various battle sites?"

Jimmy was nonplussed at the strange behaviour of this strange man. Carter noticed the boy's bafflement. "Just kidding," he laughed. "Some scrap, eh?" He pointed at the signs of butchery.

Jimmy was completely unnerved. He didn't know what to say.

"Hi, kid. I'm Harry Carter."

Jimmy then smiled with relief. "Oh, yeah. Ashok told us about you."

The man laughed. "Fame at long last!" He looked at Jimmy and pointed at the sand that covered Jimmy's vomit. "You through with spewing up?"

Jimmy nodded.

"Then come and meet the gang. They're waiting to greet you. Come on, we're just behind there." At that, Carter rose and began running, bent double, towards some distant rocks.

Jimmy hurried after him.

37

Jack, Ashok and Bill were taken to the Temple to see Panuf.

Panuf sat on his throne beside the altar. He looked agitated. He had so much longed that Shibboleth would be returned to its rightful place. He had prayed that, with its return, Vadek's position would be consolidated and that his own status as High Priest would continue. Now, not only were these possibilities highly unlikely but the tribe faced civil war. He feared that the repercussions, when the Supreme Council learned of the trouble, would be swift and merciless. He doubted if he'd have much of a future, whether as a High Priest or an ordinary Rathing. He prayed that any punishment would not entail him being sent through a Time Gate. Please, please not the Time Gate! his inner voice squealed. Panuf's hopes had vanished like grains of sand scattered by a howling wind.

He looked down at the children. He was so pre-occupied with his fears that he spoke quietly and without any conviction. "Our Overlord has other matters to deal with. He has commanded me to speak with you."

Ashok had placed Jack on the floor. He walked towards Panuf. "I know you've got a few problems,

but d'you think my friend here can have his wheelchair returned to him?"

Panuf looked at Ashok and shook his head. "There
would be little point in that. You are here because I
have to tell you that you are due to be executed
tomorrow. We have no more time to waste on any of
you."

The boys exchanged frightened glances. Each one
of them prayed that death would be as quick and as
painless as possible.

"How are we going to die?" Jack asked.

"Not by drowning," Panuf replied. "You have been
nothing but a thorn in our side ever since you arrived
here. Jago will be instructed to devise a fitting end.
After your death we shall place your heads on the
beach, as is the custom."

38

Jimmy sat amongst the group of hardfaced men and women. As members of the Freedom Fighters army (all fifteen of them), they were heavily armed. One of them, a young woman everyone called Angel, kept throwing a switchblade knife point-first into the ground. It kept toppling over in the soft sand.

"Save the knife-throwing for some Rathing's heart," said one of the men whose name Jimmy had forgotten.

They had been discussing how they could rescue the three boys locked up by the Rathings.

"You should have gone through the cave with the others when you had the chance," Angel said.

"I couldn't leave me mates with those rat-thingies," Jimmy protested.

"Very noble of you, Jimmy," Carter smiled. "And you're talking baloney, Angel. If you were in this kid's position, would you run away and leave us, your good compadres?"

"Guess not," Angel smiled back.

Carter addressed Jimmy. "We reckon that any sentence passed on your friends will be done within the next day or so. I guess the odds are against Vadek keeping them as prisoners, since he doesn't have a labour force at the moment – apart from the Droons, that is. Sure, he can mount another raid to get more human slaves, but that'll take time. I'm sorry to say, Jimmy, that on balance, we believe he will be inclined to execute the boys."

"He can't!" Jimmy objected. "They ain't done nothin'!"

"That isn't the point, man. Vadek is now facing civil war, a revolution within his own tribe. His brother leads a rebel army. He realises that he now has to fight on three fronts; against his brother, against the Magars and against us. His tunnel-extending scheme will probably be put on hold pro tem. The Droons and three kids aren't going to be a sufficient labour force. And if there's another battle soon, he won't be able to spare the guards to oversee them. And on top of all this, he'll want to end this civil war before his big bosses take steps to sort it out." Carter shook his head. "Nope, Jimmy. Vadek will want the boys out of the way as quickly as possible so he can concentrate on the big issues he faces."

"Can't you help?" Jimmy asked anxiously.

"My other name's not Santa Claus for nothing," Carter laughed. "Sure, I reckon we can give you a nice surprise present of your three pals. We've decided to launch another attack early tomorrow morning. It will be a little easier now that Garbath and his troops are out of the way."

"Thanks," Jimmy said. "You're a real pal, mate."

"Don't be nice to him," Angel counselled. "He's not used to it and he may come to expect it from us in the future."

Everybody laughed.

"OK, guys," Carter announced. "Let's mosey off to base, have some chow and shut-eye so we're all bright and bushy-tailed in the early hours."

They started their hike towards a distant cliff.

39

The boys sat silently in the holding cell. They knew that death was imminent, which was fearful enough. But not knowing the method of their execution held even greater dread. Jack, who had already been threatened with death by impaling, could not help but be physically sick. His heart raced as never before, his stomach continued to churn, and his body trembled uncontrollably. Bill was biting his finger-nails to the quick. Much as he tried to hold back the tears of terror, they flowed from his tight-shut eyes, creating little rivulets in the grime and dust on his cheeks. His bowels felt loose and squidgy from the knot of fear that lay in the pit of his stomach. Ashok sat perfectly still, resembling a wooden statue, his eyes fixed blankly on the wall opposite. His brain had closed down. He had forced himself not to imagine what gruesome end lay in store; he refused to allow the fear of the unknown to take hold of his imagin-ation. Imagination was the greatest friend of terror. Ashok was in a complete state of shock.

Time seemed to drag. Each minute took hesitant, tentative steps to join the next and the next, until they seemingly reluctantly morphed into an hour. And each hour grew larger and multiplied itself again and again and again. And time eventually settled itself besides the exhausted children and gently blew sleep dust into their eyes.

But it was not a sweet sleep the boys enjoyed. It was harsh and ragged and jagged and disturbing. The dark-grey misty darkness of drowsiness witnessed the flashes of reds and blues and yellows, of myriad colours, as the subconscious mind struggled to dominate and force the boys to realise that peace was not for them. Not now. And not in death. And that pain and agony lay in wait, and could not be ignored by the pretence of slumber.

Suddenly, their restless night was shattered by the sound of staccato gunfire followed by loud squeals and shouts. Someone in the corridor outside the cell yelled, "Behind you!" and then, "Whoopee! Got the rat!" More shouts. More gunfire. Then silence.

The cell door was forced open and a man stood in the entrance. He held a Sten gun in his hands. "Come on!" he barked.

Without a word, Ashok bent down, picked up Jack and rushed towards the door. Bill followed closely behind. A group of people stood in the corridor looking anxiously about them. The bodies of several slain Rathings lay on the ground.

"This way!" a heavily armed woman wearing combat fatigues shouted and, with the others, rushed the boys across the beach and towards the cave entrance that led back to their beach and village.

Jimmy stood there waiting for them.

"Skedaddle!" a voice called out. Ashok turned round and recognised Harry Carter. Carter saw Ashok and grinned at him. "And we don't want to see you guys around here again. No more wandering through caves. Understood?"

"Thanks, mate," shouted Jimmy as he turned and

fled with the others into the cave entrance. "I owe you one." The others joined in with expressions of gratitude.

Carter raised a hand in acknowledgement. "Toodle-pip, chaps. Sorry our acquaintance was so short." He gave them another of his big grins, waved and, with his band of renegades, ran at a trot across the sands.

"I'll give your love and kisses to Vadek," he shouted as he vanished from sight behind some large boulders.

Ashok looked quite exhausted, having carried Jack across the beach at high speed. He leant against the rock face to get his breath back.

"'Ere, give 'im to me," Jimmy stretched his arms out towards Jack and Ashok. "Let's take it in turns. I'm quite used to carrying him by now."

He took Jack out of Ashok's arms. "Are you OK, Jack?" he asked.

Jack nodded, aware that this was the first time Jimmy had called him by his name.

The boys arrived on their beach. A gentle breeze played against their faces.

"Yippee!" Jack shouted with glee, riding on Jimmy's back like a cowboy on his trusty steed and waving his right arm around as if holding a Stetson.

40

Jimmy stood beside the others, who lay on their backs, flat out with exhaustion. He scanned the beach, hands on hips. "'Ere," he said nonchalantly. "Anyone for a game of cricket?" He pointed at the cricket stumps where the boys had played beach cricket before venturing through the cave and onto Rumrunner Cove. "The gear's still there."

Jack looked at Jimmy. "Thanks for saving us, Jimmy."

"Why did you come back for us?" Ashok asked.

Jimmy shrugged. He believed it a sign of weakness to admit concern for others. So he lied. "I didn't come back specially. I was too late to escape through the cave with the others, seeing as 'ow they'd all gone ahead of me. And I was a bit fazed about going through the cave on me own, like. So I thought I'd be better off with the bird-thingies but I met that funny geezer Carter."

The boys thought Jimmy's story didn't ring true.

"Cor! What a nutter! He seems to treat everything like it's a big joke," Jimmy laughed.

Jack, Ashok and Bill began to talk excitedly about all that had just happened. Eventually, Bill said, "We'd better get home. Dad'll be frantic not knowing where I've got to."

"I bet Mum and Dad will have had the cops out looking for me," Jack said.

"And me, man," Ashok added. "Big search parties!"

"D'you think the Rathings will come looking for us?" Bill asked. "To take us back as slaves?"

Jack shook his head. "Don't think so. They don't usually take kids for slave labour."

"You're right," Ashok agreed. "They only got us because we went on their part of the beach."

Jack looked around. "By the way, where's Jimmy gone?"

"I saw him skulk off," Bill muttered. "And good riddance to him."

"That's not fair," Jack objected. "He was a great help to me when we were prisoners."

"He'll turn up again soon, making our lives a misery," Bill continued. In Bill's mind Jimmy was crude and rude, a bully and a braggart.

"He changed a lot whilst we were prisoners," Jack remarked. "I got to quite like him in a funny sort of way."

Ashok added, "And I'm sure he was responsible for saving us, despite what he just said. I reckon he saw us leave the group at the cave. I'm sure I saw him follow you and me," he said to Bill.

"He might have done so," Bill frowned, "but I don't think he'll ever change from being a bully and calling people names. He was always rude to me, calling me Fat Boy every time. Jimmy Nelson is just a waste of space."

"It might be because he has no friends," Jack suggested.

"That's his fault. And he's going the wrong way about getting any," Bill stated flatly. "Anyway, why did he wander off just now without saying anything?"

"I think it was because we were too concerned talking amongst ourselves. We kind of shut him out," Jack remarked.

"Yes, well, typical of him," Bill shook her head. "He's always got to be the centre of attention. It's always me, me, me with Jimmy Nelson."

They remained silent for a while. Then Jack said, "Look, we'd better make our way home."

"Come on, Jack," Ashok bent down and lifted Jack. "I'll carry you home."

Ashok carried Jack across the beach and towards their village. As he did so, he wondered if there could be an answer to stopping the creation of the mutant clones. The existence of Time Gates was really occupying his mind. "You know the Time Gate I was telling you about?" he said.

"You're not still on about that?" Jack sighed, not really convinced that Ashok had a viable plan. Or any plan at all.

"I really feel very strongly about this. It won't be difficult to find a Time Gate. Harry Carter knows where they're located."

"Let's say that Carter agrees to your plan. What do you propose to do once you've travelled back in time? I presume you're thinking of going back to the period in which the scientist Andersen lived?" Jack asked.

"That's right." Ashok looked thoughtful.

"Look, let's cut to the bottom line," Jack said. "Assume you find one of these gates. And assume you go back into the past and find this scientist chap. How do you propose to convince him?"

"And I was told he's a megalomaniac," Bill said. "Obviously a bit nutty."

"We'd talk to him, make him see reason. If I took

photographs of the Rathings and showed them to him, he'd believe what we were saying," Ashok persisted.

"Hey!" Bill exclaimed. "Where's this 'we' come from? I'm not going to any place over fifty years before now. No way, José. And, anyway, Rathings don't like having their picture taken."

"They needn't know," Ashok said.

"I wish you'd drop the idea," said Jack, shaking his head. "It's sheer madness."

41

Ashok carried Jack to Jack's front door. As Jack had given his keys to his captors, they rang the door bell, hoping someone would be in. Jack's mother was. She burst into tears when she saw the three boys standing there. She explained, in between sobs and hugging Jack, that she'd been at home, waiting by the phone ever since the boys had disappeared. Everyone had been desperate to know what had happened to them. Ashok and Bill left as soon as they could politely do so. They felt it best if Jack recounted his experiences without them being there.

Bill's dad wasn't in. "D'you want to come home with me?" Ashok asked.

Bill shook his head. "Watch this," he said. He rummaged about in the grass by the front door and stood up holding a key. "Emergency arrangement," he laughed. "I'm always forgetting to take my key."

Ashok said cheerio and arranged to meet with Bill the next day.

Ashok thought he should go straight home. His parents might well be in, as was Jack's mum, waiting around anxiously for a phone call from the police. But he felt that it was important for him to first formulate the steps he'd take to ensure his plan was viable. Ashok was in no doubt that the mutant clones had to be destroyed. And destroyed before they matured to their present state. The Time Gate presented the perfect means.

Whenever he had a problem to solve, Ashok weighed up the pros and cons as if he was discussing it with someone else.

So, what's your first step, Ash?

That's easy, Ashok. I'll slip back to Rumrunner Cove.

OK. And what then?

I'll hide until I can make contact with the Magars.

Yes? How are you going to do that? You're surely not going to jump up and down on the beach calling out to them?

Of course not. The Rathings would see me.

So?

I know! I'll take a mirror and hold it up so that the sun's rays are deflected towards the cliff. That will make the Magars curious, and then they'll see it's me.

Umm, OK. Fine so far.

Then I'll tell them I must see Harry Carter.

Go on. What will you tell him?

Well, I'll be well prepared; with photographs I'll have taken of the Rathings and collected data as to what they are doing. I'd have to convince Harry that, with this evidence, we should – no, *must* – go through a Time Gate and find the scientist Andersen.

So, how does this Time Gate work?

Surely a Time Gate would have to be a piece of sophisticated engineering? If so, then there would have to be some kind of device, a dial perhaps, for one to indicate what time in history they wished to visit. On the other hand, these Time Gates may be simple and natural phenomena of nature, a dimensional overlap of sorts. Whatever it is, it exists and we'd have to find out how it works. That is, if Harry doesn't already know.

All right, but why should Carter go along with your idea? Whatever it is.

Harry's a 21st-century buccaneer. He himself said it's good to buck against conventionality sometimes. What I have in mind would have to appeal to his sense of daring, his hate of the Rathings.

OK, OK. You've convinced me so far. So what's the plan?

We confront Andersen and show him the folly of his experiment. What horrors his experiment produced.

And if Andersen tells you to go fly a kite?

We hang around until we know he's deposited the embryos at Rumrunner and we then destroy them.

Wonderful. Are things in life always that simple? So you hang around. Are your ID cards appropriate for that time? What about the date on them? How do you explain that if you are asked for your ID?

Ah, caught you out there, Ashok. They didn't have ID cards at that time.

How do you feed yourselves? Where do you live? What about money? Rathing currency of the Democratic Republic of Britain will go down a treat when you try and buy a coffee.

Ashok kicked at a pebble. OK, OK. I haven't had time to solve all the problems.

So, you just want a blanket approval?

No. We're just discussing matters. Thanks, Ashok. You've been a great help.

No probs, Ash. I'll be here whenever you need any more help.

As he turned his key in the front door lock, one thought troubled Ashok. By going back in time, was it possible to change the future once you had already seen what the future was?